HARLIE HARGRAVES

Save Our King

To Lily Gray.
My bookish friend, fellow author,
and greatest supporter.

"It sucked me in by page one,
the main character Anna is fun to
follow,
and I love the other pov.
It's a great read if you're
looking for a unique fantasy."

-Lily Gray, author of The Found Us

Preface

During the early years of Thrallen, a tragedy took place within the heart of the kingdom. So great that it stalled many orders within the kingdom.

A third generation Madlock king's queen had fallen gravely ill. It was a terrible sickness indeed. Not even the court physician could figure out the cause. This of course led to panic. But many knew that this sickness could be cured by magic alone. It had been the king who suggested his queen became ill due to magic in the first place.

There are no records as to why he came to this conclusion anywhere in the Thrallen archives.

A well-known sorceress during that time had been summoned to help the queen in any way possible. She had been more than willing to help. However, when she arrived, she noticed that this illness did not come naturally. Magic brought the queen great suffering.

Which proved the king's strange theory.

No matter what the sorceress tried the queen did not get any better. That this doesn't blow over well with the citizens and dear family of the queen.

Some say the sorceress only came to further kill the queen with her devilish powers. The king was furious to learn that nothing could be done to ease his wife's suffering. It was spoken that the once bright man turned sour.

A corrupt thinking bled into his mind. Which would eventually lead to more drastic measures of rage.

Then he went on a rampage and murdered the sorceress in the grief of his newly dead wife. It was a bloody ordeal on the account of him beating her while she had been tied to a stake in Celeste Square. He even hunted her after she fled Thrallen with the help of others who did not favor the king's sudden change of heart.

No one really remembers exactly what happened after that except the close court and royal family. Whatever it may be, caused a massive tear in society within Thrallen. It forced the king to make dangerous laws.

For the next fifty years, magic has been outlawed for certain people.

No women were allowed to wield such power anymore. The incident with the Madlock queen had played a major role in the ban on womanly magic. Giving men an even bigger ego than before. As if that's what they needed.

Any woman caught with magic was either hanged by rope, drowned in the hidden river, or burned while chained to a wooden stake. They were dark times for a while.

All of this shall change dramatically when a young girl with hair as white as winter's snow strides inside the kingdom looking to gain strength and control. It has been foretold by the great Seekers. Magic will shine down upon the land once more.

It's only a matter of time.

Acknowledgement

I'd like to thank my family and closest friends for believing that I could accomplish my dreams. I worked hard for these books to be put out in the world. I hope you all will enjoy them. I thank my growing group of fans. Thank you everyone again. Until next time!

Also, a special thank you to my closest book friend Lily Gray. This new edition wouldn't have made it out into the bookish world without all your gracious help.

Check out her thriller book *They Found Us*!

Save Our King

One

Warm winds blow from the cool South, encouraging my hair to fly like a mighty dove flapping its wings. Short white strands swim in front of my hazel eyes that are dotted with lush green specks, performing as nice accent pieces.

Eyes my father said that had once belonged to my mother long ago. It is only a distant memory passing through my mind during this journey. It certainly isn't worth pondering over. I didn't know my mother.

The heavy travel pack I haul around my shoulders contains

various supplies such as a small pale brown blanket and dried meats. Several pieces of fruit litter the bottom of the bag as well. I've yet to take a moment to munch on sun-dried apples that come from a little orchard just south of my village.

A bearskin canteen dangles from a hook on the outside of the top flap. Dark green ropes are tied at the bottom. It makes a clanking echo with each step I take. A noise once annoying now turned comforting. Being alone is all new and frightening. I needed something to keep my mind focused on my quest.

There is slight excitement lacing my gut, making a small smile appear on my chapped lips.

The other bag I drag along this path holds all kinds of armor pieces, flimsy daggers, and various spare tunics I found hidden in my father's trunk. Anything I could ever need for a worthy fight is right here within arms reach.

The blacksmith in my village, Unthany, is an old family friend. Or at least that's what I assumed. He and my father would make private visits from time to time to discuss something strangely secretive. I didn't have a clue as to why they snuck around like they did. But if my father had someone to talk to when I wasn't around then it was alright.

I would not complain about his time spent away from me. I've always understood what it meant for my father to live without his wife.

Unthany was the first to congratulate me on my sudden wish to leave Coplina. He is big and tall and always covered in smoke from his shop. He might appear angry, but he is just annoyed with all the pesky requests he gets from the village. Most of our town is older folks who always end up bending their finest silverware. He of course could be tasked to fix them. And yet it seems that he did have a soft spot for

2

the village knight-wannabe. The elder blacksmith gifted me some things when the news of my upcoming journey traveled throughout the people.

I'll forever be grateful.

Coplina was a newly buzzing town after word got out. No one keeps such things from each other, especially when someone plans to leave town to seek a better living. My most favorable part was receiving a battered sword that the blacksmith had lying around his shop. A very mesmerizing event that I'll never forget. I cried myself to sleep for a week after that.

Such joyous tears I had shed. Honestly, I'm rarely the crying type.

The steel was heavy once strapped to my back in a worn leather sheath hidden away underneath my dusty yellow supply bag. It grows a million pounds heavier with each crucial step I take up these not-so-gracious hills. My thick calves ache. My muscles train with every move I make. And yet this oddly satisfying torture is worth it.

Certain thoughts will my body forward no matter what. As I imagine wielding the blade in a wondrous gory battle butterflies swarm in my plump belly. A fierce wave overtakes half of my senses. It encourages me to unwillingly squirm. I fight the urge to soothe my plush sides to try to get rid of the tingles that spread across my body due to excitement.

Such things were only ever in my dreams. Now I'm going to make them come true.

From a very young age, I knew I was meant for greatness. At least some greatness to grant me the position to leave the drafty town that gave me no real life. And now I will be fulfilling that grand mission I conjured up all on my own with the help of his stories.

And I will be damn sure to make my father proud of me and all that I accomplish.

My sweet father, Ceden Scarrow, always used to say, *"Bring more than you think you'll need, better to be prepared, my little Anna."*

It never occurred to me how deeply I took that piece of advice to heart. I still go by it to this day.

Hence why I brought along three different-sized knives and a hammer. There wasn't any room to sneak away a pair of mallets from underneath Unanthy's sinister gaze.

Ceden was a wise man indeed. Always telling me what to do and how to say certain things with polite manners. I knew it was hard since he didn't have a woman to teach me womanly things. So, I made sure to take in everything he gave me regardless of what it was. His helpful words will never be forgotten.

They are singed on the inside of my heart.

I am dead set on arriving someplace new with a pep in my step. A place where dreams come true with hard work and intense determination. Aspects I was certainly born for. It is only a matter of time to prove it.

Striding down the long path leading to Thrallen is a pleasant trip so far. Occasional pine trees line the gravel trail which provides cool shade, allowing the warm sun a break from shining harshly all day. A late spring still lingers in the heated air.

Birds sing out dazzling tunes from their tree branches. The music tickles the insides of my slightly pointed ears. I couldn't be more grateful to hear such calming sounds. They make the walk less lonely.

This mighty adventure only started three days ago and already do I know this is the right move.

I made this plan as soon as I learned of knights during my early years of childhood. My father would tell stories of how they were so noble and loyal to the kingdom. They swung their blades with such courage that the nearest waters would rumble into a thousand waves. A startling glint from their bronze breastplates could blind an evil foe in battle. Even their sacred code struck fear into their enemies.

Of course, all those tales come from Thrallen, and little me was living within another sad excuse for a land. A kingdom that isn't worth thinking about. It's old and troubled and dangerous. At least it once was. But maybe it won't be that way for long. Their new ruler may prove to be useful and caring. King Niko overthrew his father and spread the word that he wanted to give more and take less from the people.

I tossed the little ivory-colored pamphlet containing his new royal decree the moment the messenger shoved one in my hands when he came to Coplina. It was some rubbish about his new plans to improve our way of life. Funny words coming from a coward who kept in the shadows while his father performed unwanted actions upon us. The late king's tax on our crops forced a few families out of the kingdom.

I'm almost glad my father wasn't there to see those empty promises.

The kingdom of Delvina is nothing compared to the kingdom of Thrallen. A place where everyone thrives on pure happiness. A place that holds many festivals and royal parties to help the community and people prosper. I have not come across its walls yet and I already know how magical it is all going to be.

Our king in Delvina did not care for his subjects, only power over us. I have no idea how this one will be better than the last. It is a good thing I left my village when I could. Thrallen is grand and true. Somewhere that sported equality, mostly.

A good reason why I need to live the rest of my long life there.

~ ~ ~

The night before I got ready for travel my sweet father passed away from a heart attack while picking herbs in his garden. A tragic day no one expected. He was in such good health that barely any grey hairs speckled his beard. The massive orange sun had not even set fully yet. His body was recovered by the village physician and wrapped in cloths for burial. That morning everyone gathered to watch him be laid to rest within the dark moist earth. The smell of wet dirt drifted into the air. No more than a few sniffs were carried with the roaring breeze.

I didn't shed one tear or offer a hoarse sob. None of that would've done him any good, and certainly wouldn't bring him back to the land of the living.

I knew my father wouldn't want any sadness on that day no matter that he died. He was a very peculiar man. He meant for me to be strong. It was all he ever believed of me. From what I've gathered in my life, my father has seen all the potential in me that I simply overlook. Even my mother would say the same, or at least I think she would.

She has been dead for nearly ten years, passing to the heavens first.

No proper memories of her are stored away in the back of

my mind. Sometimes I feel sad that I can't picture her face. But there is no point in dwelling on that.

I am left with no one. Now an orphan only just entering a deadly new world full of bloodthirsty men. What can go wrong?

The thought makes me more upset. The moment I left on my adventure tears slipped from my eyes. Hot salty tears for my father. There was no care for what he would have wished. I could not contain that silent pain any longer. I will miss him dearly. Not having anyone else in this strange world is concerning.

Yet nothing can stop my wandering heart. This is what I'm meant to do.

So, after the wooden plaque was planted at the head of his grave, I left without saying goodbye to my neighbors. I didn't plan on giving a damn about my past from that point on. It is best to only think of my future.

The once high and mighty sun starts to set low in the blue sky. Crows begin to land around the dead yellow grass surrounding the path with broken branches. Their black eyes drag over my staggering form. I feel their sharp gazes on me. They make my skin crawl and my chest seize.

A dense forest of naked trees appears after an hour of walking wondrously up a tall hill. Just nothing large mound covered in dead foliage that does its best to hinder my quest. Towering stocks of rich yellow sunflowers act as a menacing layer to the darkness it seems to protect. Their shadow temporarily covered me from the blinding afternoon sun. My lips break into a relieved smile. I didn't know such gorgeous golden flowers grow so far north. I've only seen them very briefly among the cornfields back in Coplina. From what I've heard they flourish at the center of Delvina. Maybe they are like that here in Thrallen too.

The sight makes my eyes water from the harsh surge of anticipation that floods in my chest. I know exactly where I've stumbled upon. Thrallen will soon be in my sight.

Not a single soul has been seen anywhere on this harsh road which leaves the journey somber, calm. I should feel already defeated due to the circumstances that caused me to suddenly pursue this quest of mine. The openness to this road that winds through Thrallen lets me keep my head on a little straighter than usual. However, this observation doesn't alarm me in the slightest like it tries to.

I can't help but think of what I might encounter when entering the ghastly woods. Dead things or scary creatures must be waiting to pounce on any person who comes close. The thought of angry wolves with bloodied yellow teeth rushes into my mind. It's hard to force a nervous smile back.

No. I mustn't think of such horrid scenarios. There is no need to get all riled up over nothing. A woman on her way to becoming a knight should not feel any ounce of fear. That would simply be a step back from what I have already accomplished.

Soon I reach the edge of the wood. The tree line spans out for miles and miles. Almost creating a semicircle. I seriously glance down both ways and let out a sigh. The motion rattles my hefty lungs, giving my insides a furious tingle.

"Don't freak out," I mutter to myself.

Two

Horrifying screams spill out of the trees and soar into the air. I jump back with a sudden blast of fright that races through my stubby form. My shaking hands itch to grip the small blade hidden inside my right boot. The heart in my chest pumps fast as I observe the border between the woods and the empty field. There is nothing remotely scary or troubling in sight. Unless I count all the barely living grass and various holes in the ground. How strange this is.

So many thoughts run crazy in my head. I can't seem to figure out if it is a good idea to go into the woods to find whatever made the scream or continue down the path. Of course, going after something that offers potential danger is never the right choice. On the other hand, a person or animal may be in serious trouble. I wouldn't be the true me if I didn't at least briefly go and check it out. What harm can be done?

Just after a moment more of thinking I take off in a strong march towards unknown dangers. My bags jingle away from all my various things clanking around inside. Fear isn't what I feel within me. Only a sense of adventure. And that is what I will forever need.

~ ~ ~

The wind flowing within the woods is somewhat different. It's not cold but not perfectly warm either. A grand sign of glorious spring. Beams of gorgeous gold sunlight cascade down in waves lighting up everything around me. Funny how this place appeared gloomy from the outside. But inside here is fantastic. An absolute beauty. I'm glad that I'm not afraid.

My large round eyes scout ahead to take in everything around me. Anything that looks unnatural should be easy to spot. I have only ever seen normal things. My greatly willing ears strain to pick up any sounds or noises that might be linked to something amazing.

My breaths became slow and controlled. Staying calm is the ultimate strength I can muster now. If I freak something out, then I'll surely panic along with it.

My thick legs take me down the ever-going trail. The deeper I go the darker everything quickly gets. The fading rays of orange light quickly slip away. Almost as if great magic calls upon it. To make sure it all arrives home for the growing night to blossom.

Even the trees seem to be encased in a gloomy sheen and their sparkle is not yet lost. Almost like shining stardust. Not that I even know what that substance looks like. But I can sure try to imagine such a sight.

The bright sun disappears too soon. I can't help but wander slowly over to a tree that's a few strides away from the path. Something strange catches my intrigued gaze. Giddy chills flush down my spine.

A new feeling I acquired once I first stepped foot out on the road leading away from the village.

Oh, how amazing it remains. It refuses to leave my being. I never want it to flee.

The tree's trunk must be twenty feet in height. Massively lanky as well. Also, very round with a shallow hole right in the middle.

With a careful step forward, I search the inside and only find an empty nest that once belonged to small birds long ago. Spiderwebs spread out all within the cubby hole, creating funny-looking curtains.

The craftsmanship used to create this unique webbing is wonderful. The silk strands glint in the dying light.

Some might be disgusted with the sight or weirded out, but I know it to be beautiful, and daring. The way each string is intricately woven together is truly whimsical. Sweet time had been taken to form such magnificent artwork.

I won't dare ruin a poor creature's life's work. There is not one icky gut in my curvy body that would destroy anything that isn't bad. That puts me in a different category from every man. Nothing in me will convince me to harm innocents.

The dark gray bark of the trunk shines with the disappearing light. This is the first time I'm seeing trees. My village isn't exactly covered by anything other than sharp little shrubs. It has never rained enough over the centuries to keep trees alive.

That place I never really called home had been encased inside a vast cornfield. The only constant crop that grows every harvest time.

With no warning, another shout sings into the howling winds. It's as if the woods stand still like a lake that has no breeze blowing across its frozen surface. All noises have vanished into oblivion. No sounds remain other than my racing pulse. It may be heard anywhere. It thrums in my ears wildly. The sweat echo of my heart is ever so enticing.

I decide to act and follow where it shot from. Not the smartest idea I've had today. Though that won't stop me from going deeper into the woods anyway.

After a few moments, I realize it zoomed from my left off the dirt path. Now, there is a subtle tick of doubt that shifts within my mind. I very well could lose my way and never find the direction back out. Now that is an awful thought to have. An unwanted shiver shoots down inside my stomach. An ice pick of curiosity tries its best to sway me fully into motion. I fight the urge to puke suddenly. But I swallow down the bile that rises over my tongue.

Stay calm. Nothing in this forest can hurt you, I chanted silently to myself.

Somehow, I don't believe that at all. And that's what gets my blood pumping.

~ ~ ~

My steps are stealthy like a black cat with light feet. Snapping a twig underneath my feet can alert anything or anyone of my new hidden presence. I peer out into the consuming darkness, mimicking the movements of a hoot owl. Not sure what exactly I'm looking for, but I'll know it when I see it.

Nothing alarming is in sight so far. Just pale white aspen trees. At least something is familiar to me.

A light chuckle erupts from me as I remember that these very trees were what my father once craved to see in person. He read about them in a borrowed book long ago. He deserved, no, my father needed to see them. Sometimes they were the only thing he would talk about when not telling me those stories.

I was never given the chance to ask what was so special about those trees. Too late to find out now. I can only hope he's surrounded by them in the place above the highest clouds.

The deeper I go the various noises become stranger. Low growls and quick snarls. Though the source cannot be determined just yet.

After a while longer I stumble upon an open area with a bunch of jittering men dressed in the most lavish clothes. Too pretty for them to be simple village folk. Their faces seem to be lathered with a pale green sludge. I think it's some kind of mud. My nose instantly scrunched as if I can actually smell it all the way over here. As I squint my eyes, I can see that it is in fact different shades of mud that had been smeared all over their exposed skin. Thi is very bizarre. Disgust makes its way inside me.

The small clearing starts right at the end of a branching path connecting to the main trail. Quickly, I hide behind a thick tree to keep myself out of sight. My heart thumps madly, almost like pelting rain over a wood roof. I fear that if it speeds up then it will surely jump out of my chest.

"Did you see the size of that boar?" One man asks another, maybe to no one in particular. He sounds rather pleased with himself. I can tell by the evident smile in his tone.

A few chuckles and snorts are made in response to him. A small shiver of curiosity laced with caution flies down my spine.

"Hah! I've seen many other things that are bigger." Another makes the foulest moan I have ever heard. There was no doubt that it was meant to be sexual. They all scream with horrendous barks at this person's words.

I shake my head at their weird mannish behavior. Brutes they must be. Like the boys in my village. They always hunt for sport and never put steaming meat on the dinner table. That's the only reason my father killed the small creatures found in our naked shrubs back home. Tiny things covered in barely any fur. However, none of that matters now.

Carefully, I step away from the trunk and attempt to flee when, unfortunately, I accidentally crush a fallen branch with my hasty step. A wicked snap fills the forest like a terrifying shout. A slight hiss flutters from my throat. Just fantastic. Why am I even surprised?

Fuck, I curse to myself. A nasty swirling of my gut makes me heavily cringe. I briefly cover my mouth to hold back a nervous gag.

Suddenly all their wild calls and grunts stop. I cause no sound or shift to get away. The possibility of making things worse is not very appealing. Nothing happens for a few moments until a strong voice speaks openly into the trees. A very captivating voice it is, almost calming despite the force behind it.

I'm beginning to think I'm in real deep shit.

"Who's out there? Come out, slowly, with your hands raised high." The voice commands me. It is full of unknown power. I have no choice but to listen. My very life might depend on this one moment.

I know from my father several things. The most important lesson I learned can now come into play. Don't look like a crazy person doing crazy things. Meaning coming up with a believable story is a good way to go. Let's hope I can say something useful.

I start to move again, turning back around and walking from out behind the tree to face the men. My chest rises and falls rapidly. I can't tell if this is the feeling of excitement or fear, perhaps the difference matters not.

My packs suddenly grow too heavy.

"Didn't mean to step into a private hunting party." I keep my head down making sure no eye contact takes place. I'm practically burning holes in my boots from my intense gaze. I am not built for such hurried exchanges.

Best to keep my mouth shut and force down any confidence that tries to flood my body. There is no need for me to act all tough. That just is not in my deck of old playing cards today.

"Well, look what the deadly woods decided to bring us." A man jokes and follows his words with a sickening whistle. I don't care enough to settle upon his boring features.

My hands tremble at my sides. I grew up with most of the girls and boys back home, so meeting new people is different and scary. There is no bone in my large yet short body that gives me the strength to want to meet new people in secluded spaces. This is more frightening than the dark parts I have seen so far in these woods.

I find comfort in such darkness. It never hurts me, and it

15

never will.

Loud footsteps start to approach me. Panic settles in within my thick bones, but I hold my ground and don't move a single muscle. By now the warm breath from whoever it may be fans across my damp forehead. A nasty shiver rakes down my spine for the hundredth time today.

Whatever is in this forest makes me sweat and gives me chills. I hate it and want more at the same time.

"Are you lost, girl?" The man whispers. The same one who ordered me to show myself in the first place. He sounds even more dangerous up close.

"I heard a scream." That is all I can manage to say.

I can't say the real reason why I ventured out into the woods. I'm on my way to the kingdom of Thrallen to illegally join the Knight Trials and claim my dreams.

A competition made up of three different tasks to prove who is destined to be a true knight worthy of Thrallen. Just thinking about it makes my heart jitter.

The stranger speaks softly into my ear. "That's what really captivated you in these wicked trees? Who are you, girl?"

I want to badly run away, fall into a deep ditch, and slowly die from embarrassment. Of course, a young girl like me with rare curves and white hair walks into the woods because an insane scream tends to raise red flags. People of any sex would ask questions and wonder aloud.

For a moment I search my highly active brain for any possible answer that won't sound off or unsettling. I have never been any good at making conversation with any person other than my father. Well, not for the reason of being shy. I rather like my alone time. Maybe it would've been a good idea to learn people skills before starting my quest.

"My name is Anna." I keep my tone bland, uninterested, careful not to intrigue this man more than he already is.

"Well, Anna. Call me, Lord Kasper." The man, Kasper, backs away carefully. His friends snicker at whatever actions he commits.

Must have been quite funny to them all. Their horrendous laughs are not pleasant to hear. My skin crawls over my muscles and tendons like wriggly worms. I suddenly want to run back into the deep trees.

I do a ridiculous bold thing; I peer up finally. I instantly meet the purest of ocean-blue eyes. Never have I seen any type of ocean or large body of water before but if I had to blindly describe one, it would be the color of Kasper's eyes.

His hair is a dark sandy blonde color that curls slightly at the ear, creating a mop atop his head. A small scar graces the corner of his top lip. He might have been injured long ago. He is rather tall. He looks somewhat close to my age. Though it is easy to tell Kasper is the younger one of us. Grand red robes cover those broad muscular shoulders. Gold thread trimming the fabric. He is a very thick man indeed. A lot different from the twig-sized boys in my town.

Suddenly, I feel even smaller than usual. Damn, this Lord Kasper and his amazing body and face cause strange emotions to ram through my chest. I don't like it one bit. I have to get out of here before things get worse.

I'm not bad looking either. I've got a slightly round face with constantly flushed cheeks and a slightly curved button nose. My curves, rolls, and soft skin probably symbolize that I'm the perfect female to birth massive babes for beefy men. I will never be a thin goddess in my lifetime, and I'm quite alright with that.

17

But maybe once I become a knight, I'll gain a good number of muscles.

"Pleasure to meet you, Lord Kasper." Instinct takes over and I give a sarcastic bow.

I don't want to appear as a frightened child with no idea how social status works. I've lived like the lowest in the power chain my entire life. It's not my first time being told that a lord is in my presence. Plenty came to the village to demand our season harvest. Evil crows they all were but not this one in front of me now.

Lord Kasper displays a pleased smirk on his lips and turns to give an amusing look to his friends. They each are different in many ways. Though they all are tall and very muscular. It makes me wonder if they're knights. It's not that far of a stretch.

"You must seek Thrallen." It's not a question. At least Kasper isn't thick in the mind like his large frame. He's oddly serious as he scans my form for any possible threat.

I gaze intently at the man once more and declare he isn't to be trusted. Pretty men like him get what they want with nice words and plump sacks of gold coin. I won't be a girly fool and fall for his little show. I don't have the patience to be belittled either.

Without one more word, I bend down for one last time at my waist, infusing more flare into my bow. I even expose the back of my neck. Then I turn to walk away, leaving Lord Kasper and the rest of these men in a shocked state. Their open stares hit my back. A small smile of triumph spreads across my face the further away I get.

Three

Another hour has passed before I find the path once again. I honestly don't mind the walk. It's nice to take mental notes of all the different-sized aspen trees and their strange twirling branches. Great admiration sparks inside my heart at finding one single connection in this journey.

Those men are now far gone in the distance. I no longer worry about one of them growing too curious to follow me.

Everything is going so well until something hisses close behind me. This time I waste no energy in being as silent as possible. With a hard snarl on my lips, I jump around to come face to face with a massive green vine with thousands of thorns attempting to wrap around my ankles. That hissing noise comes from the leaking holes it's covered in. They act like a thousand tiny whispers.

The sound makes me twitch.

"Shit!" A curse word seeps off my tongue as the enchanted plant manages to trip me.

I land right on my backside with a loud thud. I'm met with harsh twigs and sharp rocks pressing into me. A huff is all I can make out. The plant keeps coming after my feet for whatever reason that I can't come up with in this moment. It's actually terrifying. Tears of quick terror spring to my eyes.

So much for being brave, I instantly think.

I hurriedly back away. Dirt flies out from my rushing feet. My boots clash against the ground roughly. My wide eyes scan every inch of the forest floor to find something to defend myself with.

That's when a brilliant idea pops into my frazzled mind.

Such a grand plan it is. My gaze lights up in wonder.

In one swift motion, I strip my pack off my back and drop the other bag that is filled with armor to my side.

A massive weight left my twitching body. The only possible weapon that is left now is this old, dented sword. The glint in my eyes grows red and a glorified smile springs on my face.

This is what I've been desperately waiting for. I can finally put my dreams into action. All I can wish for now is that my father is watching this.

The terrifying vine that leaks a nasty red sap that smells like rotting flesh keeps snapping at my toes, but I'm somehow faster. I gain a few feet of slack and manage to get far away enough to stand back on my sore feet. With great movements, I raise my arm and clasp a hand onto the cool leather-wrapped hilt.

It's hard to ignore the crazy amount of weight that is the decent-sized sword. I pull the weapon from its worn cover, raising it high in the dusty air. This is what glory has to feel like.

As if a bell goes off, a stream of golden light seeps into the canopy overhead to shine down upon me. Like the gods, Seekers, above recognize me in this moment. Maybe it might have been my mother and father watching over me, making sure I have the strength to defeat any foe that comes my way.

I don't even realize that I've spent the entire night waltzing through the woods only to encounter such terror in the early morning.

A massive wind blows from all directions creating a vortex and making my hair and leaves fly wild. A dangerous roar echoes around the area but there isn't time to question the source.

"Come get me, bitch!" I must be strong and brave. My voice, however, isn't loud enough to make a sturdy front. I sound like a little girl who's afraid of the big bad dark. Somehow after everything I'm still not scared.

The evil creature lunges at my right leg. I try acting smoothly by swinging the blade down onto the vine. It withers from the small slice I give it. I gasp at the sight of more red sap bleeding from its bright green flesh. No matter being injured the plant continues coming closer and closer. It's on a mission to get me at any cost.

Where does it come from? I must think quickly.

From what I can barely make out, the very end of the magical plant slithers out of a hole in a distant tree.

That's where the source of its life must be. I then jump out of the way when it moves to wrap itself around my waist. I break into a sprint all the way to the tree and only trip and fall on my face once.

Bright red blood slips down my face while I stagger the rest of the way up to the tree. I give one look back and see that the vine notices that I'm no longer in front of it.

It whips around and instantly spots me crouched down next to the tree facing the hole where it dwells, slithering in its sickly sap. The thickest part of it rests just inside, I can't find where it ends or how deep this dim hole goes.

"Hope you've had a wonderful life." I sneer while rising from my spot and lifting the sword above my head.

Before it can fully reach my right thigh, I harshly bring down the twisted blade with all my womanly might. I chop clean through its meaty column. A grave squeal echoes into the forest around me. It drops suddenly like a limp leaf in a heavy downpour of cold rain.

It's silent for the rest of the time I linger here.

With exhaustion heavy in my bones, I sit down next to the remains to wipe my greatest weapon clean. I have never had the chance to use a sword before. The brutish boys in my village during our earlier years would play with wooden swords and harmless bows and arrows. It was never in me to ask to join their grand battles or maybe pretend to be the maiden in distress.

Now, with the still-warm blade resting on my lap, everything becomes more real to me. The path is only inches away from where I left my packs. Thrallen is so close I can practically taste the Knight Trials in the slightly moist breeze.

A tremendous adventure this had been, leaving home to go find a foreign kingdom. To fake my status and gender seems wild enough. The rest of the way through the mystical forest is perfectly calm and deliciously silent. No more groups of men or dangerous plants have come out to greet me. It's only me and all that I own.

Soon the end of the long path is revealed. The different assorted trees look to be alive. Beautiful green leaves cover their branches to form waves of color. The air is sweet with the scent of earthly energy. A bright ray of sunlight lights up the ground.

A sigh of longing escapes me as I take in the sight of a tall wall-like border out in the distance. For years I wondered what the edge of Thrallen's main city looked like. But now glancing at it from afar causes wild thoughts to fill my mind. I start to question if I can really do this.

It's real. I made it to the grand Kingdom of Thrallen with almost no problems. The feeling of triumph would be so much greater if my father were here to soothe my ill mind.

Not only will I have to falsify my way into the trials but also survive them. If the image of upcoming battles doesn't frighten me then the possibility of being caught sure does. I can't be simply caught. I must depend on myself now to get this just right.

Not because I'm a young woman posing as a nobleman. I have the one secret that can get me executed with no hesitation by the king. Either by burning on a stake in the town's square or drowning in a fierce cold river.

I possess the gift of magic and am about to enter a kingdom where powers like mine are forbidden for women to have.

Danger lurks just beyond these walls. In truth, I go hungry

for the taste of purpose.

Four

The walls of Thrallen are a lot different than I thought they'd be. I pictured them to be a polished dark brown, not this patchy gray color like they are now. Or have checkpoint towers at almost every glance I take. These weren't in any of the stories.

It doesn't take long to arrive at the massive gates. The doors spring up like giants, creating a mysterious plague to sweep over my heart. Not something I need right at this moment.

What awaits beyond these beautifully carved doors must be my destiny. The very destiny my father foretold all those years ago in our crippled house. The greatest challenge I will ever have to face is so close. I feel it within the tips of my fingers.

So damn close indeed.

I think of my father, wondering if he would be proud of me for only glancing over the carved bears in the royal crest with whimsical sunflowers caressing them. Sunflowers are Thrallen's signature flower, every kingdom has one along with a certain animal, like the grizzly bear. That the simple inhalation of this legendary air will be enough even if I chicken out and run back to Coplina.

A crest that me and him drew for many years on spare pieces of parchment. I'd know it anywhere in this vast world. It swarms my various dreams and consumes my very soul almost. It's engraved in my simple spirit. This is it.

I raise my hand, my fingers trembling as they hover over the wood. Before I make contact, the doors are pulled open by a mystical gust of wind.

Hot and pulsing magic swirls intensely inside my chest, magic that isn't mine by a long shot. The gates have been enchanted with perfect ease. The only power I've ever felt is my own. This is much older and darker. I shiver at the jerking shock it gives me.

I quickly notice hundreds of townspeople skipping along in a big hurry. Excitement graces their faces. Their smiles brighten the streets. Children run around with playful bows and arrows, pretending to strike a killing blow with wooden swords. Fake shields clash against each other along with their extraordinary laughs.

I spot two beautiful, golden-skinned women holding hands and gazing into each other's eyes as they walk down a market. Their love can be seen by anyone and admired by anyone.

There is an older man sitting down on a stool outside a small café sipping a cup of steaming tea gently. He's having the best morning possible. A few others sit around him endorsing plentiful conversations about their day-to-day lives.

So many happy people in this main town of Thrallen. It's everything I could have imagined and more.

A pang of remembrance flakes in my mind. I wish my father was here to see me become a knight. We could talk about my days in training or how it feels to be a respected member of the knighthood. He would have adored this place. He needs to be here with me. It's all I will ever want besides Thrallen robes.

Fabric banners of yellow and brown scattered ropes going from house to house. Different colors of shredded paper had been scattered on the dusty ground. The town is enormous with giddy folks, horses, cats, and dogs running alongside one another.

My feet carry me down the market. I stop to look over a few booths that snag my interest.

First, I glance over the unique kinds of animal hide in the first booth. The next one is full of wonderful jewelry. I think of how the ivory pearl necklace would sit upon my neck.

Even I wonder what all those frilly dresses would feel like on my body. A foolish peasant girl's biggest dream or perhaps nightmare depending on how I'm looking at it. But it's not either of mine. I'd much prefer a hunky set of new bronze armor that the Thrallen knights wear than a nice gown or two.

I can't picture myself as pretty and don't plan to.

A burst of delighted screams jolt from behind me where I stand close to a little cart selling canteens. I carefully place the small bottle I was holding back down and give the booth

27

owner a gentle smile.

My eyes openly watch a group of city folk center around an ugly man. His bald head pokes out on top of the crowd. He must have stepped on a stool. The poor thing lacks any decent height.

I casually approach the far end of the group, eager to witness what the royal messenger might say today. Those yellow robes he wears make his ivory skin shine green. His red mustache is severely messy. A nasty sight he is. Does he present himself to the king in such a manner? Gross.

Somehow, I resist the urge to gag at his ugliness. I notice others struggle the same way. Good to know I'm not the only one who finds him repulsive.

He clears his throat before announcing rather loudly, "I am Coven, the royal messenger as most of you should know already. I've come to say that our new king has decided to give his first speech two hours from now on the stage in Celeste Square. The grand speech will concern his rightful duties and the information of the Knight Trials since many of you have been demanding answers. Now, the trials tent is still mounted up just one street over. Quickly sign away if you wish. It will close at dawn."

After speaking with one deep breath, Coven struts away and leaves the people and me in a buzz.

Now that I know the location of where I'm meant to sign my name on the Knight Trials' official documents I can be on my way. I practiced my manly signature for weeks, all for this moment.

After glancing around to spot any possible prying eyes, I carefully walk away, and down the road Coven said the tent is on. There are sparkling nerves thumping inside my round belly.

It is the first creation I spot. A large brown tent with trimming of gold that has a small line of people waiting to write their names on the roster.

A new sight to my eyes indeed. Tall and buff men, men of noble blood. Things that I'm not, nor possess. Yet it does not cause me pain to see the aspects I missed out on. Most of these fellows are covered in mucky dirt. No one is really put together in a clean sense. Most definitely need a long soapy bath. Suddenly, being a woman is not looking any terrible.

I gaze everywhere around me, searching for any sort of space secluded enough to change my appearance. I can't approach the tent as a full-on woman. That wouldn't be very wise, I'd certainly cause a scandal.

A new resident (WOMAN) of Thrallen mistakenly wanders into the Knight Trials Tent. I can already see the headline of the kingdom's public message column. Even though the opposite gender can be rather clueless sometimes.

They wouldn't even know that I would've walked in there on purpose. My pretty face would surely erase any kind of trouble running my way.

There's a nice little abandoned shack at least a hundred feet away. Maybe there is a door in the back for me to sneak inside. Without a moment of thought, I'm wandering away in a simple walk. Keeping a low profile hasn't been so hard. Now the only real task is to keep up the façade.

It doesn't take long to arrive around the other side of the shack. A broken door at the back is all that blocks me from getting in. With one last look to catch any spying folk, I tumble into the dim shack.

Many holes litter the top letting bright sun rays flow down, giving plenty of light to cast about. I hurry to launch my packs down on the dirt ground. Then I start to sift through the bag with all my small supplies, trying to fish out a small canister of smudgy black dust and a brown cap.

Once my fingers touch the cool lid of the tin, I hoist it up to open it in a shaky rush. Dark dust erupts from the sudden movement, flying up into my nostrils making me sneeze.

I quickly pause, refusing to make any sudden moves. Fear that someone heard my noise echoes into my chest. Though no one comes to discover me inside the shack.

I'm in the clear for now. There is no more time to waste.

It doesn't take a long while for me to transform into a short man. All dirty and chubby-like.

I used the dirty black substance and a little broken paint-brush to draw a brushy mustache above my plump lip. The shining lid of the tin offered a great reflection. I make my eyebrows connect in the middle, giving myself an uneven unibrow. My hair is securely pinned underneath the worn cap. I guess it belonged to one of the village elders back home. There was no way to tell since I found it in the street on a random Tuesday four years ago.

Next, I shove a small pillow underneath my shirt to create the illusion of a mead gut. It works like a wonderful charm. No fool will suspect a thing.

Before gracing the world with my new manly presence, I dig around and pull out a sheet of yellow paper and a silver stamp. The items suddenly bring on memories of the early start of my journey to Thrallen.

~ ~ ~

"Will you do this one thing for me?" I asked the blacksmith, Unthany, if he could create a unique seal. This was the fifth time this week I sought him out just for this simple reason. Something he wasn't too happy about hearing again.

"If anyone found out I crafted an imposter noble seal, you will receive all blame." He had told me. There was no other way he would create such a thing. That was his one true condition. He wasn't going to do anything without it. I knew this.

"That I can take. Not being a knight would be worse than any punishment ever be given to me." I meant my truth. I swore upon my mother's grave.

That was weeks before my father passed.

I then went to the village bookshop not too long after talking with Unthany. "Can you write out a noble document for me?" I questioned the owner of many books. The old woman named Agathen had been bound to have seen such papers already. Nothing new to be put in front of her eyes.

"What's in it for me?" The woman asked me. Her white brows twisted in question. Though a slight tinge of curiosity sparkled in her pale brown eyes. I smiled at the sight.

"After I become a knight, you will receive a small bag of gold and silver coins every six months. That alone should allow you to buy a new shipment of books and other materials. Surely that would make your shop more popular?" I had this plan sorted out for many years.

Kept track of the best people to turn to. To entrust them with my secret. I knew this was just the kick to have dear old Agathen cave in.

"You got yourself a deal." The lady said just before rough drafting the parchment based on my wickedly clever ideas.

As I gaze upon both items now, it becomes set in stone.

I will be known as Lord Mason of the Triscan house. From a faraway land near the western border. No one will ever know the truth. Or so I hope.

~ ~ ~

The walk back to the tent isn't so easy this time. I make my figure straight and tense, covering my large chest with my pack while carrying the other.

The line of men has depleted savagely. I'm the only person left other than the little secretary sitting on a bright yellow stool with a scowl on his rough face. This should be fun.

He gazes upon many different documents. Though his head shoots up at the sound of my heavy steps. He doesn't seem too enthusiastic about my presence.

"You're in luck. The last slot will be filled by your name, papers if you will." The man sticks out his hand, expecting my nobleman papers, to scan, check, and examine for accuracy.

I give them to him cautiously. The official house page, a document about my supposed house's livestock, and a large drawing of the Triscan seal. I silently thank Agathen and Unthany for all they'd done for me. None of this will go to waste.

I stand patiently, not breaking a sweat, it is terribly nerve-wracking. I can't afford my unpredictable emotions to lash out now. Definitely not today.

His beady black eyes shift at me, peaking over his thick spectacles. "Everything seems to be in order." He shows his broken yellow teeth. As if he were smiling. I suddenly want to hurl at the gross sight.

Once my newest belongings are taken back and placed in

my bag I bend down, taking a blue quill in my shaking hand.

The stem of the feather feels all wrong in between my fingers. I know now that this is against everything a knight stands for. That these various lies are dangerous. Maybe someone will understand one day why I'm doing all this.

The signature I sign isn't my own, it belongs to Mason Triscan, the fake me. It feels odd to see the messy writing. The risk of the name being too perfect is greater than I would have liked. This is the best option. Be as unbalanced as any man would be. Seemed like a good idea at the moment.

"Congratulations, you joined the other three hundred men waiting to fight in the Knight Trials. Good luck, Mason Triscan. I'm sure you're going to need it." He gives me an unwelcome sneer. That does not ease my upset stomach. Neither does his act of shooing me away like I'm a pesky fly.

I give him a silent farewell and leave the tent, breathing more harshly than ever before. Everything around me is beginning to grow lopsided. It's difficult to stand up straight. My whole world quickly spins around horribly.

In a quick second, I steady myself against the shack I manage to walk to. I have more important tasks to worry about than a surprisingly weak spell.

The town's people are running around in lines going toward the square. Some women are pulling along their husbands. Others rush in small groups. Everyone is excited about the King's speech. I think I am too, or I will be once these nerves calm a little.

There is no time to wipe off the dirt around my mouth and brows. So, I go along with them and join in the fun, dancing at their sides as if I'm one of them. It's a temporary feeling.

We all parade around to blissful tunes, singing an ancient

song that I do not know of. It makes warm feelings flow from my heart and down into my feet. My toes clench fiercely in wonder. My cheeks are set on fire from pure glee.

Then we arrive at the square, a sinister hush washes over us.

A huge dark wooden stage is perched at the back. Big posts hold up a golden canopy. The kingdom crest is patterned at the top, giving enough room for the main people of Thrallen to get a good glimpse of it.

I'm right in the middle, getting a perfect view of the waiting king. But he is not just the new king. I've seen this man before, but where? I step on the tips of my toes to get a better look. My eyes go wide when I realize who it is.

The newest king of Thrallen is no other than Kasper, the man I met hours earlier in the deadly woods. Those ocean eyes are not so easy to forget.

Five

The magnificent crowd cheers as one glorious voice. Their hands are raised highly in the later afternoon air, waving around to get the king's attention. Though he seems more interested in straightening his mighty robe, drapes of soft yellow and chocolate brown, embellished with gold thread. A bear crest rests on both shoulders. Many rust-colored tassels hang from the thick cuffs on his arms too. So pretty. So royal

King Kasper's crown is made of pure gold. A bright green gem has been embedded right in the center of the twirling designs. Made to look like a glorious flame. I wonder why. What was the reason behind it?

The crown has been passed down from king to king for many centuries. I stare in complete awe, watching the yellow and orange sun make it shine, creating light in little streaks across the canopy. His whole being glows in power.

This is how I picture a grand king to be. It's surprising to know that I already met him. He wasn't so tough and stern in the woods. Kasper was just a lord then with an arrogant fluff about him. Not the unbothered king he is now.

There is one thing we are soon going to have in common. I will also lead another life to escape the one I was given.

I don't feel so alone after knowing this.

A deep throat clears from behind him. The king shifts to his left to reveal a dark figure who's standing at the far edge of the stage. His face is surrounded by a black hood. I can't see his features that well. The mystery man slowly walks forward to whisper something into Kasper's ear.

Whatever it is knocks Kasper back into reality.

His blue eyes go wide as he takes in the sight of hundreds of people sporting smiles, all of which are for him and his speech. The suddenly skittish king shuffles up to the little stand. A royal crest was branded into the shiny wood as well. It's been built for this speech.

"Hello, people of Thrallen!" His voice booms across the stage. Everyone goes still. No more words are spoken. As if their voices are snatched away by sudden amazement.

I lean forward due to an odd tug in my chest. It is familiar yet unknown. It sings to my heart. I recognize the tinge of magic in my mouth, the same power that opened the gates hours earlier.

A sour tang clings to my tongue tasting of green apples. So strong that I force myself not to collapse in a heap. A gag pushes its way up my throat, but I know better than to let it out. My body wants to violently shiver.

Every person's magic has different feelings. No magic wielder is the same in Seekers Land. That information was taught to me in secret by my father. Even though magic in Delvina is legal he still wanted me to hide in case one day I did leave for Thrallen.

Whoever has been casting unspoken spells surely feels strong and dark. They know how to command their power to do the most damage.

Not someone I want to ever encounter.

"You all have been waiting for this speech for some time now. I'm here in this very moment to deliver just that." There's a slight tremble in his deep voice that makes him look younger than he is.

No one seems to notice his fear but me.

The townsfolk go wild, jumping in the air like crazy birds. Some accidentally push others forward. Those people land atop others. A truly rowdy crowd this is.

However, I'm not paying attention to him anymore, but the man behind the king certainly has caught my interest.

I can't see his face clearly. Dark shadows swirl around which makes it hard to seek out his eyes, hiding beneath the cloak to keep himself a secret. Not wanting anyone to see him. It encourages me to be even more intrigued. Not a good thing to feel. I really should ignore him and focus on the king.

I look around for any possible way to allow the light to shine upon him despite my self-given warning.

A smile pokes at my lips when I see a torn piece on the

canopy that covers the stage. It won't take much magic to tear it open just a little bit more. There can't surely be no harm in trying. So, I will go for it. There is no hesitation within my stomach this time. Which may be terrible for me.

With one swift flick of my wrist, I let a sliver of power ease out. It's been swelling inside me all day. I hold in a gasp as I mentally guide the gust of my magic all the way up the stage steps. The feel of it slithering up is rather pleasant. The sliver of power is connected throughout me. Somehow, it links in my hands all the way to my toes. A smirk tugs at my lips. The need to concentrate on the task at hand lingers in my chest.

A shocking flavor of rare cinnamon coats my taste buds. A unique spice only the rich can keep in their stock. That's what my simmering power tastes like, nice and sharp. It's like the very juices consume my swelling tongue.

My father always hated it when he could feel me using magic around the house. Not because it was horrible. He only hated how I could never control how much I let out. He may not could have tasted or smelled my magic, but he just knew when I wielded too much. Of course, the trembling cups and shaking house were also big indicators. Well, I almost have a great hold of it now.

Drops of hot sweat slip down the sides of my face, causing the brown dust of my brow to drip slowly down my terribly glistening face. I'm grateful no one has noticed.

It takes much effort to not create a visible form of energy. Some folks can sense that. Though most magic is invisible to non-users. Some, however, possess the Eye to see such things. Only they do not get to wield magic.

My magic reaches exactly where I want it to. I close my eyes, keeping my slightly raised hand steady, careful not to make a show out of it. Then the stray piece of fabric rips back further. Yellow rays seep down inside and form a halo around the dark man. It's a surprise no one is watching this happen.

They're all too busy waiting for the king to gather his strength to finish his wonderful words. No one makes any negative jabs at him for his nervousness. At least that's what I think it is. It's easy to see how much weight is on his shoulders.

I don't think anyone truly wants the burden of ruling a kingdom.

"My father was a kind and fair king. I will do my absolute best to be like him. You all have my word." The king lifts his arms, commanding a flow of screams and shouts. The people appear to love him dearly.

No one else pays any mind to the figure I'm trying to uncover. As soon as the light appears more smoke with odd strikes of bright red sparks constricts it, choking it. Then he's suddenly disappearing right before my eyes. The taste of his power overwhelms my senses completely. It's a miracle that I can keep on my feet. What the shit?

My jaw drops in a not-so-subtle way. A few moments later he is gone. He's a gust of wind that blows out a yellow candlelight. He isn't next to the king anymore. I search everywhere for him. He's not even in Celeste Square from what I can tell. Where the Seekers did he go?

This has to be my sign to forget about it and move on. I shake my head to get rid of the curiosity that briefly took over my being.

I can't dare worry about it now. The king motions for the people to calm down again. His excited expression becomes serious. This is the moment I've been waiting for. The time is here.

That dark man is no longer in my mind.

"As you all know the Knight Trials haven't taken place in more than thirty years due to magical mishaps." A few people nod their heads knowingly while others hesitantly drift their eyes around.

"There hasn't been a need for these competitions till now. I've received word from a hidden source that Pucnasia is planning to march onto these lands, our lands. Their ruler, Queen Pearlina, has made it known that she's seeking revenge for the loss of her daughter." Others mutter to themselves about this. The king briefly gulps. A nervous trail of sweat goes down the left side of his face.

"An unknown child supposedly killed by my late father King Dragoona Madlock." That's what sets the true horrors into the air around us.

Many gasps and cries fill the square. The atmosphere is now tainted and foul. I feel suddenly out of place. I wasn't expecting such close talks among these people. I've come so far only to forget that this kingdom is so close-knit. I think I'm losing my touch.

I'm not one of them to truly understand what this means. Not yet at least.

His voice is full of painful power. Maybe a hint of fear as well. I watch with wide eyes. Somehow, I know this is serious. These competitions are not meant to be brought back just for the fun of them. But word had spread of their resurrection many months ago. So far, they reached my old kingdom. I wonder where else the news traveled to.

What is going to happen with Pucnasia, I ask myself.

All I can do is listen to his words get more and more shaky.

"She is wrong. My father would never harm a child. H-He

was not my grandfather who killed people for sport. I won't let this q-queen ruin his legacy. These trials are important for this kingdom. I need strong and loyal men to fight an upcoming battle. Our very lives depend on this war. The lives of our women and children need our best efforts." Silence.

The silence is what consumes these streets, only echoes of birds fill the newly made void. King Kasper stands there tall and looks into everyone's eyes the best he can.

I'm absolutely terrified. All I'm here for is a silly dream. But these people who signed up for the competitions are here for a greater purpose. Men are born for such purposes. To either impress their furious fathers or get in good favor of the king.

Nowhere near am I prepared for such things. A battle for the very soul of Thrallen is a total shock to me. Can I do this? Of course, I can. I'm Anna Scarrow.

Soon women, men, and children start to leave the square. Kasper stays there for a long while before retreating into the grand white and gray stone castle at the back of the square. Colored light reflecting off stained glass windows lit his walkway, illuminating his crown and grim frown. His pace is rather on the slow side. Everything is shown through his body language. The tension in his shoulders is rough to look at. I then hope he will somehow overcome his internal battles.

It's time for me to leave as well. The need to find a place to stay and fast before the taverns and pubs are filled to the brim with guests fills me quickly. It's also a good idea to think about his speech while I hunt for lodging.

Six

Most of the lodging here will be taken up for the Knight Trials. So, I then go on a hunt for shelter with a confident smile.

After cleaning my face, letting down my white hair, and putting my little pillow back into the bag, I spend the rest of the afternoon searching for a spare room. Anything to house me for a few weeks. Long enough to even make it through the first trial.

It seems as if I visited every pub and hotel there is in Thrallen. Which I'm guessing I did. I even had to ask a few locals about places they know that are kept from outsiders. Everything is to be occupied. There may be nothing left. But then luck finds me.

I want to give up and just crash into an empty barn. It's a miracle that has come my way. I stumble across the Yellow Piggle. My shoulders sag from exhaustion and relief at the mangled sight of the tavern.

It's an old rustic pub located at the far west wall. It's a deserted joint. I can't hear any loud voices from the inside. A crappy wooden sign with a faded yellow pig hangs loose above the faded wood door, dangling from twisted chains, screeching away from the early night breeze.

Though I'm too tired to care for its limp appearance. Anything has to be better than sleeping in a ditch. I quickly rush inside before anyone notices me lingering about. There are maybe three really drunk fellows who sit in a corner tossing coins into empty mugs. Shouts of amazed pleasure from their game fill my ears. Isn't it a little late to be fussing around like this? The sight is not terribly unpleasant. I find it rather nice.

Then I spot a massive beefy man covered in glorious tattoos behind the bar shining glass cups. The ink swirls up to the underneath of his thick neck. His eyes are dark and creepy like he has no soul. I can't help but shiver as I start to approach him, nerves are eating away at my insides.

This man does not seem very welcoming. But it's worth a try. The only option that's left for me. I must try.

I clear my throat and do my best to stand straight. "Got any spare rooms?" My voice is meek. I hate how small I sound. Though it really can't be helped. Thrallen men are surely crazed-looking. A few others like him wandered the streets before the sun had set. None of them offered friendly expressions when our eyes briefly met.

This brute leans forward and sneers brightly, giving me a sight of surprisingly pearly white teeth. Though his attitude doesn't come with anything bright or cheery. I'm not really surprised about it either. I don't expect to be welcomed with open arms. That would be foolish.

"No rooms available for anyone. Especially for you." His thick accent reminds me of those who would raid neighboring villages.

They'd pass along the corn fields with sacks full of goods. Enough to where they did not stop to take more. Only to taunt me and my town. Though the memories aren't as troubling whilst thinking upon them now. So, I push them back into the far corner of my mind to concentrate on the task before me and secure a room without trouble.

"Does that mean all the rooms are taken?" Another question leaves my lips. I dramatically search around the tavern for any guest who appears to be staying the night, making sure to shield my eyes from invisible rays of sunlight. Hmm, I don't see any. Well, by the look on his face, I must be irritating the tavern man.

I just can't seem to leave things alone. No wonder why my father hated it when I asked so many questions. It isn't in me to play nice or to be serious. I should fix that before it truly does get me in trouble. Now I can understand why I always managed to gain strange looks from people.

"Get lost, girl." Oh, he is going to be difficult.

It's not hard to see that all his rooms are in fact empty. There would be way more people in this tavern if they weren't. The extra space and lack of customers prove it greatly. The Yellow

Piggle is nowhere near popular in Thrallen. Perhaps it's due to this mean asshole who acts like he's the owner. I feel no pity for this jerk.

I drop each of my bags one by one onto the long counter-like table lined with stools. A hefty breath full of tiredness shoots from my mouth as I peer up at the man.

A dangerous glint blurs my vision for a moment. When was the last time I ate something?

"Please, I need a place to stay for the Knight Trials." Maybe a mention of that will improve my odds.

"What does the Knight Trials have to do with you?" He slams a recently washed glass down onto a red rag. It makes a squishing noise. I squint my nose in disgust. Noises like that encourage my innards to roll.

I'm already prepared for these sorts of questions. My father made sure I had every possible response memorized. Just in case someone was catching onto me not being in the right place such as the trials. There is no room for snooping peasants while I'm trying to become a knight.

"I've traveled far to watch these legendary contests and bask in the glory that is man. Will you truly deprive me of such wishes? Hmm?" With a flick of my lashes, I'm sure I get under his skin. Though I hate acting so fond of such creatures. Men aren't all that great. I experienced that firsthand today in the woods. Gross is the proper term for what they seem like.

Disgusting pigs who are only good for one thing, silver and gold coin.

He stands there watching my breathing. I fight the urge to run the other way, to cower beneath the stairs towards the back like a frightened child. But instead, I decide to cross my arms and mimic his stone form. It's not a good idea to mock this man, and yet I find it absolutely thrilling. The blood rushing in my veins proves that I'm doing something wild and free.

This is going to be fun.

After a little while his face softens. There is no telling what will happen next.

"You stay until the trials are over. Then you shall be on your way home to whatever village spat you out, girl." His eyes narrow down at me.

A thrashing grin breaks across my face. I stick out my hand for him to take. He grips it tight and gives it a harsh squeeze.

"Then it's a deal." I nod. Feeling overly triumphant.

Seven

Crowlen

My day was going great for the first time in a long while. Though I knew that eventually, bad luck would find me. And it never lets me down. I should feel honored that it has stayed at my side for all these years.

I had actually been excited to witness my close royal friend and superior give his first speech as king. I was a proud warlock for the most part. I had even helped the young man write his speech during the late hours of the night that led into the early morning. Then of course something foul had to fucking ruin everything. It was like clockwork. I'm never given the chance to experience simply joy brought on by happy things.

There was no surprise to flood my guts.

I was rather thrilled by the new chance to lash out. Bad things always happen to me. I might have even thought a curse was placed upon me. Now that does make the most sense.

If that were true, about the whole curse idea, then I wouldn't try so hard to be normal. Of course, people like me aren't lucky enough to feel any ounce of normality.

Everything ran smoothly until an incident at Celeste Square happened. I didn't even get the chance to smile even a little bit. These dormant muscles hidden beneath my skin weren't granted the chance to flex into a small grin or a slight frown. A robbery has occurred, my glee stolen.

It appears that there is an unknown thing out to get me. I thought all threats to me and Thrallen's crown had been eradicated long ago. Maybe it is time to start the Witch Findings again. Those always made my sour mood turn sickly sweet.

Receiving the go-ahead to hunt folks who aren't registered as magic wielders in the very act of using magic was an amazing feeling. I had witnessed fear scratched across their faces as I shoved them inside the dungeon cells to be tried surely gifted me great pleasure. Though, those days had long since been gone. Shut down to all the violence I caused for the past three kings. I haven't had the need to form a hunting party in decades.

In an instant, I appear in the royal throne room after being attacked by horridly muddy magic. The taste of a strong spice still lingers at the back of my throat. Instead of puking up everything in my stomach I take a deep breath and swallow the taste.

A familiar tinge of anger coats my being, my internal flames threaten to burst free from my palms. A snarl forces its way onto my thin pale red lips.

Someone has tried to reveal me, a deadly move on their part. As if the people don't already know what I look like. It wasn't formed to where the Royal Warlock is meant to be hidden away. I enjoy walking down the cobblestone and dirt streets without my hood to strike fear into their hearts. The people know what I can do with my magic, they don't need further demonstration other than my sinister red eyes.

I take great pride in how the people fear me. They also know I'm here to protect Thrallen and its king from harm, meaning they too are included.

It must always be this way. I owe it to myself.

A person in the crowd wanted a first look at me, meaning a true outsider of Thrallen craved a glimpse at my glorious form. I wasn't ever going to give them that satisfaction.

I'm not by any means a simple man. Never was and won't ever be. They will just have to leave.

Dark clouds roll around my angered form. My pale hands twitch, influencing sparks of red fire to fling into the dusty air around me.

I'm absolutely furious. I'm the only magic wielder in this city. No one other man is documented for such gifts. When I first came here, I was ordered to test everyone in Thrallen for any sort of power after the incident occurred. This is definitely someone new. And I fucking hate the very idea of that. Makes my bones grow weak with utter disbelief. No one will make me out to be a fool. Over my dead body.

I pace around in deep thought, attempting to piece together why a woman with magic would show up. Unless she is dumb enough not to know the truest law of Thrallen. Magic has always been complicated for bitches, excuse me, witches. That is the only reasonable explanation. Females from other kingdoms do not have to hide magic.

So why would one show up here? Something doesn't feel right. I feel all types of wrong right now. I think I'm going to really puke.

My slow-growing peace is rudely interrupted by a harshly breathing Coven. The short balding man skips into the throne room with an aggravated eye. Poor thing was kicked in the face by an unsettled horse hours ago. The black eye only just now is beginning to turn purple and blue. I may or may not have enchanted the beast to do this. I felt the need to make Coven leave me alone for a while.

Of course, that did not work out too well since he's still in my damn line of sight!

A smile graces my lips. I roll my eyes in the most obnoxious way possible. I'm not in the mood to hear this giddy pitter-patter for the hundredth time today. Nothing in me wants to hear his pestering.

"You vanished quickly." Coven decides to point out the obvious. What an imbecile. Whoever sent this little wimp my way better be counting their days.

"Yes. The stench of cinnamon ruined the moment." I say in a low tone. My deep voice is laced with tension. I don't bother to stop my eyes from rolling again. Such a nasty habit

I formed from all the years I've spent with King Kasper under his late father's rule. This didn't seem to upset the other man. Nothing causes the little rat to run, unfortunately.

Coven chuckles. "I assume you don't really mean actual cinnamon. That's a little too strange, even for you, master."

It's like I need to curse this man into Pucnasia. Anything to get rid of him. Perhaps I should call upon the town's pest exterminator.

I give him a crooked smile. The corners of my mouth curl up to reveal white sparkling teeth, some come to a sharp point, showing exactly which line of grand beings I came from. If anyone truly knew about my lineage then war would break out in Thrallen. Best I keep my mouth shut.

A sinister idea comes to mind. Something rather nasty.

"Someone in this kingdom used magic upon me. I'll hunt her down and kill her. I don't care how it's done."

The mental image of me tying a frail old woman of a witch to a wooden stake shoots a thrill down my spine and into my cock.

Damnit!

Eight

I quickly learn that this ginormous man who owns the Yellow Piggle is called Artis. He did not like it when I bashed him with many questions as he led me up steep steps. All the way to a cold hall with doors lining the walls. Walls covered in truly ugly purple paper with green flowers. It must have been years since this place was decorated.

I silently take note of what I would like to change when he isn't looking. Maybe move some potted plants into the hallway to give this place a new tone.

A smile grows on my face when he shoves open the first

door we approach. Artis grunts for me to go inside. He is a man of little speech it seems. I do just that with a subtle hint of excitement.

A small twin bed was pushed against the wall, covered with a thin orange blanket and topped with an even skinnier black pillow. I'm very glad to have brought my own to use. Not that these are bad. It's just that I have extra to really get comfortable.

This place is the size of a large closet. Maybe like those in the castle filled with glorious dresses and shoes.

A lone window lets brilliant moonlight cascade down into the room, lighting everything up in a pretty silver-blue glow.

I gently place my bags next to the foot of the bed and turn to face Artis.

The owner of the Yellow Piggle watches my every move closely, being properly cautious about my strangeness, not that I honestly mind. Of course, he would be worried about my odd arrival. There is no blame in my heart for this.

It is expected. A good way to act indeed.

"Thank you." I slowly offer out a dirty hand to him. I inwardly cringe at the sight of my nasty fingernails. Dirt and juices from that killer vine out in the woods still cover my knuckles as well. Not a pleasant way to look. I didn't think to even clean myself up before running around Thrallen like a loony person.

Artis studies my slightly shaky hand. Maybe he's pondering on if he should indulge in my foreign yet welcoming touch. He sighs while clasping my hand in his overly massive one. His fingers cover my dirt-coated flesh completely. Everything about him is massive. It frightens me very little. I feel everything but fear.

A giddy squeal comes rushing from me.

"You will not regret this. I won't be in your way. You won't even know that I'm staying here." I go silly with excitement, jumping on my feet like a child.

"Don't give me your word yet, kid." Artis yanks his hand away and leaves me leaning against the door frame with a ridiculous grin plastered on my heated face.

This is going to be wonderful. I can feel the impending success way deep inside the marrow of my thick bones.

~ ~ ~

For the rest of that long night, I empty each bag and find places to store my stuff in. Then I make the bed with my extra blanket and tiny pillow. It doesn't take long for this place to get cozy.

Though it will never be home. I really never had one. It died along with my mother and father. It's sad to think about really. But there is no time for it. I shake my head free of the image of my father's gentle smile and pretty green eyes.

I lay upon this little cot and stared at the ceiling, counting each crack, and inspected the wood, welcoming the lumps that met my back.

Sleep does not find me until the truly late hours set in. I think I dream of swords and mystical plants.

But a frown seems to be permanently set on my face. A distant fear settles in my big heart. But I can't figure out what it may mean. And that only fuels it.

Nine

T he next morning trudges on by rather hastily. A familiar crowing from a rooster wakes me without using too much effort. My back aches from this dreadful bed. I now have a crick in my neck. Maybe staying here won't be so great. None of that matters. It's the only option I have and that has to be enough.

I'm up on my feet and dressed in a simple day's garment, common clothing for common women. No one will suspect anything to be wrong with me. Well, there really isn't anything wrong with me on the outside besides my striking white hair and abnormally plump body.

I did get the occasional stare from thin vultures that call themselves noble ladies when walking around town to find a vacant room. Or maybe they were prostitutes waiting to meet a lonely fellow and got angry for me stepping on their turf. I can't seem to see the difference.

I just have secret magic to worry about. No big deal.

I do sport a nice brown skirt followed by a dark blue tunic with long flowing sleeves tucked into it. However, it's tough tying the gentle front corset strings. My large breasts are squished for the simple use of fashion and modesty, making it harder to breathe normally.

I look like a sweet innocent village girl. Nothing like a brutal knight that I will be. The thought is somewhat odd. I have often daydreamed of how I'd be in a full suit of bronze armor.

After lacing my boots, I glide down the stairs only to have a mouthwatering scent rapidly flood my nostrils. A real nice delight this is indeed.

I find a plump woman with salt and pepper hair rushing in and out of a swinging door. I figure there is a small kitchen back there. That's pretty obvious.

The lady notices me standing off to the side. Her dull blue eyes go wide. She gives me the most brilliant smile.

"Oh, you must be Anna. I'm Aunty Kurty, a pleasure to meet you." Aunty Kurty quickly embraces me in a tremendously tight hug, her large arms caging me to her. I have no other choice but to return it with the same amount of force, as I had been compelled to do so by her cheery energy.

"Um, who are you supposed to be?" I ask with a hesitant glance around the very empty tavern except for those fools from last night and some other people I don't know. They sit at the far back table and seem to be continuing their silly drinking game.

A few early birds are scattered around various tables, two sit at the bar with plates of hot breakfast sitting in front of them. From the smell, it must be thick pancakes and fresh pork sausage links. They're enjoying their early morning meal like clockwork.

Out of nowhere, my stomach growls loudly, and instantly a flash of heat builds up my neck and onto my face. I haven't eaten anything in a day or two, which isn't the best strategy to become a knight. I was too busy worrying about the trials and King Kasper to feed myself.

A shame that is. I can't believe I let my rations go to waste. They have to be soiled at the bottom of my bag by now.

"Well, I'm the wife of Artis. The finest tavern owner in Thrallen." Aunty Kurty is full of pride for her husband and his place, sounding almost as if she expects me to already know this. I hate to say I had no idea this tavern existed until I was aimlessly wondering upon it late in the night.

"That sure is nice to know," I say with a quick nod. "Where is Artis?"

Aunty Kurty ignores my question for the moment. She gently grips my wrist in his pleasant warm hand, three rings adorn her fingers. She leads me over to the first stool she approaches. I take this as a sign to sit and wait for her words to hopefully explain what I'm apparently missing.

"It's a Monday. Artis is out hunting for mushrooms in the woods. The usual really." Aunty Kurty tosses her hands in the air as she speaks. I duck back a little, afraid she might whack me.

Aunty Kurty begins to whip up something special behind

the bar on top of the counter where I can't see. I can tell that whatever it is will be tasty. The sweet smell hits my nose just right. My stomach loudly roars as Kurty places a bowl of softened oats garnished with blackberries in front of me.

I catch the drool that managed to dribble down my chin before taking the curved spoon Aunty Kurty offers me.

"Thank you," I say with great enthusiasm that I don't have to fake before digging into my fresh meal.

Soft groans of satisfaction slip away from me. I can't help myself. It's just so damn good.

"Nonsense child. It pleases me to know we have such a youngling staying with us. Even if it is for three weeks." I lower my next filled spoon at that.

It would have been a good idea to make a certain schedule for myself for these three Sundays. I should have given myself small assignments to keep myself busy during the days before and after the trials. After everything, how could I have not planned so far ahead?

It is as if that important information has been lost in my mind. Thank the Seekers for this lovely woman. I would have completely forgotten if it wasn't for her.

Aunty Kurty continues to piddle around, cleaning ale mugs, folding washcloths, and chopping herbs to refill the many jars that line the wall behind her. All I do is sit and eat in silence, crafting innocent questions to ask her about the trials. Hoping that she will answer them.

Once my deep bowl is finished, I push it forward. Aunty Kurty takes it and quickly gives it a rinse. I clear my throat nervously. Kurty places this black pot, used for stewing, onto a drying rack before shifting her eyes over to me.

That delicate stare makes me want to cower in a corner.

I've been wanting to do that a lot as of late. There must be something to help get me out of that need to flee.

"Yes?" Kurty asks.

"Where would those men train for the trails?" I start off slow.

Kurty thinks for a second, her left pointer finger tapping away on her soft chin. "Why, at the Knight Training Grounds, of course. A big green field just beyond the royal courtyard. There's a sign placed at the edge to let children know not to play close to the weapon stands. No one can really miss it."

I listen closely to each word, casually picturing myself on the grounds with my borrowed blade in hand. I mentally draw a map of the town, making sure to remember every detail the best I can. I even feel my eyes light up in wonder. I wonder if Aunty Kurty notices the glee building inside me.

It will spill out any second.

"Maybe I could snag a look at a sweaty knight recovering from a sparring match." A faint blush graces my cheeks. It's rather nice to think of some hunky knight with perfectly curved muscles that gleam with slick liquid.

It feels great that Kurty laughs along with me. Good to know this woman isn't too old-fashioned to hate a sense of humor.

"You could try. But a few square folks got their eyes on those knights. So harshly that they will scare away any other female who comes by. I'd stay away from those who've been claimed. You can tell who they are by the women who linger during their practice matches." Kurty gives me a powerful wink.

Interesting, I mentally note.

Sneaking away to the training grounds might be a great option. The first trial is going to be archery. I've never held a bow or touched an arrow in my life. This is literally new territory for me. There was no chance for me to try and learn any of those skills while growing up. I was put to work in the corn fields with my father as soon as I learned to walk.

Good thing I snagged a pamphlet of the trial details as they were sent across the lands by horseback. Weapons will certainly be provided if men don't have their own. All I desire now is access to anything I need and pure silence. No eyes will discover me in the dead of night. It's the perfect cover.

At least I hope so.

"You look like you need to have some adventure in your day." Aunty Kurty stops fooling around and wipes her hands on a white cloth.

She reaches into the front pocket of her white apron and pulls out a small brown pouch. The sound of thick coins thrashing around makes my eardrums tickle. I quickly stand off the stool as Kurty stalks towards me. In a rush, I shove my hands out in front of me, telling her this isn't anything I need from her.

She's done enough for me already. "You mustn't give me coin. I have none to repay you back with. Surely you need it more than I." This is true.

Somehow, I managed to convince Artis to give me three weeks to provide payment for the room. That was the only way I could guarantee money. After I survive the trials and gain bag upon bag of coin, I will certainly give him what he's owed. And the bookstore owner in Coplina. That's the plan.

Aunty Kurty scoffs. "Hush now. I'll give you what I wish to give." She doesn't allow me the chance to skip away.

The bag of gold and silver coin is already shoved in both my hands, my fingers forced to grip it tight.

"I'll repay every piece back." I don't want to take it, but I feel that arguing will do no good. Kurty smiles brightly anyway.

"Just go out and buy yourself pretty things. Maybe even a new dress or two." The woman does not hide that look of disgust towards me, glancing down at my not-so-pretty dress. I blush from embarrassment; a fierce fire heats my cheeks.

The woman shoos me away and out the door. I don't have a chance to gripe about it. Kurty pushes me all the way out into the street. People are already up and about doing their daily tasks, and kids playing around as well.

I'm greeted with a beaming sunray down upon my head. The pub entrance slams shut behind me, I flinch from the loud noise. Kurty had made her wishes damn clear.

There is no turning back. So, I start to walk back into the heart of Thrallen. A smile full of optimism on my face.

~ ~ ~

Everyone seems to be bursting with joy. There are no sad faces or cries in the gently warmed air.

A few dogs chasing cats race past my feet every so often. I only laugh at their silly animal behavior.

Everything is exactly how I pictured Thrallen's people to be. It's a miracle that I'm even here among them, walking down these glorious streets, gazing at the many different colored homes. They have no idea of my true purpose.

I'm having such a lovely time walking down the streets, filing in between a wave of nice folks was a dream come true.

So many booths of dresses and breeches are scattered throughout the town. I figure that each street was built to cater to specific goods. I must have stumbled upon the one made for beauty and wealth.

Though everyone looks happy just glancing around. Only those with a true desire to shop would even purchase a gown. It's hard tearing my gaze away from sparkling jewelry. Many colors flash about such as red, purple, and yellow. Small crystals catch the light that makes rainbows.

I find a beautiful dress hidden at the back on a rack of one of the booths I approach. A black bodice with red and purple threading formed into graceful swirls. Clusters of beaded flowers line the neckline and bottom trim. The material is soft underneath my fingers. I'm very drawn to everything it is and can be.

I shift around to pull out coins when the shop owner abruptly stands up tall, she straightens her back and peers behind me. I don't know about the change in mood. Do I even want to know why this booth owner is offering a tight smile or why sudden beads of sweat trickle down her wrinkled face?

But eventually, I turn around and notice a familiar dirty blonde man dressed in the finest hunting clothes. My guts flip like crazy.

Though his being is not the only one who frightens me. It's the one mysterious man right by his side that scares me deeply. I feel the power he pushes out of his being. It's hard not to get down on the ground to heave uncontrollably.

Standing next to King Kasper is a gorgeous man with the palest skin. His tone could be a perfect match for my hair. Though his locks are thick and black as a raven's feather, strands that glow blue in the sun. They lay down on his chest and back in slightly curled waves. He too is clothed in breeches and a simple tunic. A few buttons are undone to show off his pearly chest and a tiny bit of dark hair. However, every piece he wears is black except for his blood-red boots.

They match the color of striking his eyes. I think my knees are threatening to collapse from under me.

I instantly know that this is the very man who accompanied Kasper on the stage yesterday evening. He was the one to cast such strong magic that almost gave me a heart attack. The same mystical energy I felt at the city gates too. I silently wonder if he tasted my magic too.

If his power is that strong then he would have no trouble sensing mine. Fuck.

After the king said his 'hello' and 'thank you' to his subjects those ocean-blue eyes land on me. Like a butterfly drawn to the sunlight. Somehow I find that thought to be a little warm for my taste.

Fuck me, I curse to myself. There isn't an opening for me to run away.

Kasper ushers him and his cold friend over to me. I slowly put the dark dress down and bow in the best possible way. I have never done such a thing until now. So, the movements don't look right at all.

"Anna." The king says my name with a large smile. A blush rushes to my cheeks for the third time this day.

"I did not realize I'd be seeing you again." He doesn't hesitate to grip my hand to place a searing kiss on my soft fleshy knuckles.

I grow cold from the strange contact. Not because I find Kasper's touch unwelcome, but because his friend's stare makes my skin crawl. His gaze cuts me like a dagger coated in frost despite his clear ability to wield flame.

"I am only here to witness the Knight Trials," I say the same lie I gave to Artis. Well, thinking about it now it's not really a lie. I am here to witness the Knight Trials. Hopefully, he'll believe it too.

King Kasper's grin spreads wider. "Didn't take you for a groupie." His chuckle is like calming music. Marvelous tunes whistle into my ears. My heart flutters.

Though the man next to him doesn't find any of this amusing. Kasper follows my troubled glance to the brooding man.

"This, my darling Anna, is my dearest friend and royal warlock, Crowlen. Don't mind his bad attitude. He's like this every day of the week." The king pats the back of Crowlen's shoulder roughly, forcing the stone-like man to jump forward a little. Crowlen groans from pure annoyance.

Definitely not interested in anything having to do with this conversation.

A curious bubble seems to have burst within me. I find myself admiring his lean muscles that hide underneath the black attire. This isn't the right thing to ponder over. I force those strange thoughts away with a slight shake of my head.

It's already bad enough that I must try extremely hard not to let my magic out. Even now it's called upon itself to mingle within my hands, pressing against my inner shields to let loose into the world.

This powerful man near me is making all my power go wild. So much for keeping cool in Thrallen. I got to keep it together.

"Pleasure to meet you, Sir Crowlen." I give him a bow as well. He's not interested whatsoever. That notion is not welcoming. I don't want to be around someone with no bright bone in their body. And he appears to be the biggest downer of all.

Kasper clears his throat. Seems as if he's noticed the change in mood around us. "We best be off. Can't keep the wild boar waiting for our arrival."

The king tugs his companion away after giving me a dashing

wink. I chuckle while Crowlen rolls his eyes. What an odd warlock. Why does he let himself be dragged around by the king?

I decide that I'm not going to cross paths with him again. Over my dead body.

~ ~ ~

I do in fact buy the black beaded dress and another in that same design but different color scheme. Blue and gold the other one is. The prettiest things I have ever owned. All thanks to Aunty Kurty.

I wander around the kingdom, taking in every entrance and exit beside the main doors. Knowing where to run is a great idea. Just in case I get caught using magic. But I don't think my outlawed abilities will ever have to be used again while I'm here. It's important for me to not indulge myself in whatever curiosity floats my way.

I refuse to screw up my only chance to gain knighthood.

There shouldn't be a reason to risk my life if I stick to myself and dwell in the shadows. All I'm here to do is become a knight and fight for the Madlock family. Can't be too hard. Can it?

I don't give myself the chance to ponder on every possible path that I could have chosen. I'm only focused on the present one I've settled on.

It's not long before the high sun starts to sway in the sky. The afternoon has started its approach. I soon slowly walk back to the Yellow Piggle. My feet ache and my chest throbs from my harsh breathing. The new amounts of pollen in the air aren't what I'm used to, it causes my allergies to swell.

When I walk inside the now-crowded tavern, I see Kurty

and Artis arguing behind the counter. It appears to be serious. Maybe this isn't the best time to come back.

Without drawing any attention to myself I carefully turn right back around, only to stop in my tracks after hearing certain words. This is definitely not a conversation I'm meant to hear.

"You cannot grow attached to that pesky girl. She cannot be trusted." Artis gripes at his much shorter wife. Not daring to care about who listens in on their very bizarre conversation. No one inside the pub cares to notice this. It's a strange sight. Artis must bicker with his lovely wife all the time like this. That's really the only explanation I have for it.

"And why not? I haven't any babes of my own. I will grow as close to her as I please." Kurty stomps her foot before throwing a dish towel on the ground and struts around to greet me and my gaping mouth.

Her smile is absolutely genuine. Something dear me can never muster after experiencing such an intense argument. This woman is something else.

"Did you have a nice time, Anna?" She asks me while tucking white strands of wispy hair behind my ear. I pray to the Seekers she doesn't notice the point of them. If she does then her thoughtful grin gives nothing away, acting as if their whole display never happened. Artis goes back to wiping down wood tables. He's completely normal again.

"Yes, I did." A shy answer is all I can muster.

"Good. I'll have supper ready in an hour. Go wash up dear." Kurty guides me to the stairs, not giving me a choice to stay behind and sit at the bar to relax for a moment.

With dresses in hand, I do as she says and go up the stairs and into my room. I carefully place the black one into a dresser drawer and keep the bright blue version out. I'll wear it down to supper to show it off. This puts some good use to what I used Kurty's coin for.

It's a shocker that the gown fits around my generous curves. As if it had been made for me. Not many plump girls my age grace this world. A true blessing this is for me.

I attempt combing my hair with dirty fingers, getting rid of knots and flyaways. Next time I'm in the market I shall seek a comb. I make no stops for ten minutes. Not until I feel herself presentable enough. But when Kurty calls me down for supper, I have to give up my quest to appear pleasant.

There are no other shoe options for me. After placing my travel boots on I skip downstairs with a light pep in my step.

Kurty made a delicious rabbit stew full of carrots and radishes. I never had such a tasty meal before. My father was not a great cook. We normally stuck to having stale bread and cheese. Maybe even having several stocks of yellow corn when the village had leftovers from harvests. There has been enough of that to have fourth helpings some days.

Our food choices aren't the reason as to why I'm on the plump side. My father was a hefty man with soft chubby features. I can see where our resemblance was from. I also believe I inherited his trick for being sensitive to old or new injuries of others.

At the bar, I sit in utter silence. Each spoonful of rabbit in my mouth and into my belly makes me sleepy. It has been a while since I ate a decent meal. Just as good as breakfast. This woman is going to fatten me up more than I already am.

Once done I slide the bowl in front of a waiting Kurty. She watched every bite I took. Like she gained happiness from me enjoying her meal. That makes a question pop into my head.

Why don't they have kids?

I can't find any nerve to ask.

The woman smiles before taking it away to give it a thorough wash.

I take this as an opportunity to sneak away back to my room where I can wonder about these colorful people in peace.

Until darkness blooms across the sky I'll stay inside and when no one is around I shall take my leave once again.

Ten

Crowlen

I really don't want to do anything on this particularly boring day.

Yesterday's events are still hot in my mind. Whatever witch decided to show her magic rattles my bones in the worst way. Now is the time to plan out a search for her, to create the appropriate punishment. Not to go out and mess around on a hog hunt. Damn this Kasper and all his ridiculous schemes.

The king dragging me into the town is rather annoying and

completely unfair. All the laughs and smiles are really terrible to witness. So much happiness. So many glorious souls. It makes me sick.

Vomit might spill from my throat the longer I have to shoot people my stare of death, or warning, depending on how they perceive my gaze.

Though my only friend doesn't seem to mind greeting the people of Thrallen, it's his job. I just hang back to watch the bright interactions pass by me like cold winds. I want nothing more than to turn back to my dark chambers to wallow in my permanent gloom. Being away from people is all I desire.

"Come now, Crowlen. Just have a giggle or two. No harm will come to your preciously dim mood." Kasper nudges my shoulder in a friendly manner as we pass down the street full of wandering women looking for fancy clothes, hunters looking for new hides, and children playing with stray dogs and cats.

I can't help but roll my eyes.

Then my king gets furiously dragged away by pesky ladies who want a share of him. Their filthy laughs command Kasper to grin. The need to sneak away is heavy in my mind. To leave the town. But there is a powerful shift in the afternoon air that rattles my bones.

A slight twitch in the air and I'm almost collapsing on my knees with shaky breaths. What the hell?

I'm quick to scan the area around us, making sure my king is well, but Kasper hasn't noticed this like I have. Good. Nothing truly alarming catches my gaze. I know I'm not just feeling false energy.

And yet when I land upon a curvy woman with pure white hair and a dashing smile my lungs fold in on themselves. My body has no idea how to react. I feel faint.

A precious woman with voluminous hips scans as many dresses as she can. Silently, I admire the way her fragile hands caress the dark gown she inspects.

The color will pair nicely with her pale flesh. I instantly shake the random thought out of my head.

Harshness takes over my stone features. Then in by doing so I accidentally snag the eyes of the shop holder. The old woman stands tall, allowing the mystery girl to grow confused.

Don't look at me. Don't grow curious enough to turn around. I can't see your eyes.

Is it possible to lose one's mind when a woman I don't even know turns around to peer at my king? Her eyes do not fall on me first, and for that I am glad. But they do drip over clueless Kasper. For some reason, this angers me. I shove down the feeling deep inside my gut.

I haven't a clue as to why I feel so depressed when it wasn't me this mystery woman first locked eyes with. I'm going soft. Kasper should just kill me now and let me rest in the fire pits below our feet.

Never have I been interested in girls before. Sure, I've had my fair share of whores who warmed a bed with me in brothels down in Buskav. However, no woman has dared to approach me and I've been quite fond of that notion. But her lack of attention for me is getting under my skin. I hate it. I hate her.

Kasper of course can instantly notice her raking over him. He tugs me over to her in a hurry. I bit my lip to keep a complaint from spilling out of me.

Then he introduced her to me, and I think my heart jerked a bit. Hearing her name was almost orgasmic. Anna. Such a beautiful name for a girl with dashing hazel eyes.

Yes, I believe I must have tripped and fallen on an exposed

tree root and hit my head very hard. It's the only explanation as to why I'm suddenly interested in a visitor to the city.

I really don't listen to their slight conversation. I'm far too busy looking anywhere but at her round face, flush lips, and heated cheeks. Her stunning yet youngish expressions force my stomach to twist.

However, my attention switches to her after Anna explains she is here for the Knight Trials. That alone shakes any weird possibilities out of my mind and allows an interesting thought to appear in its place.

Perhaps I should start my search with the folks who have come to watch the trials. That's a good start to my investigation indeed. I should thank this woman and her words of inspiration.

My skin grows hot with anticipation. The small hairs on the back of my neck shoot up when mine and Anna's eyes lock for a split second before Kasper leads me away. Whatever is swirling behind those green and brown orbs is strange and new.

Hmm. That gives me another idea that I must not share with anyone.

Eleven

The dark navy-blue sky creates the perfect cover for me to carefully make my way to the training grounds. Even the usual roaring winds of these lands have died down greatly. As soon as I went back to the room, I changed clothes. I now wore tight brown pants and a loose dark green tunic, the sleeves engulfing my hands, comfortable enough to move properly.

The bright yellow and orange lanterns hanging from posts lining the streets are wondrous. I recognize the warm glow of these flames. A wordless spell of the simple magic wielding.

I'm not the least bit surprised that Crowlen's power extends to the little details of this city. It's clear that his magic is grand and wicked, much different from the wild tendrils that call my soul their home. Sweat most likely doesn't break across his brow when he casts a charm or says a spell. Mine is not very in tune with me. Sometimes I can create a small wind to wrap around my being with minimal effort, other times I fall into a deep sleep after failing to light a candle.

My father didn't understand why I could not call upon it like most magic wielder he knew of. Not being able to get a grasp on it frightened him. That is what encouraged me not to reach into my heart to use it.

Whatever power I possess moves on its own most of the time. I haven't the time to try and corral it into my open hands.

No one is out currently. All are either sound asleep or partying in taverns like there won't be any tomorrow. Though the thunderous music that comes from nearby pubs makes the night less empty.

I carry my bag filled with armor and all that I need. The sword is hidden behind the back of my shirt, I securely strapped the sheath around my shoulder and above my breasts. Its cold steel creates goosebumps to flare on her skin. I welcome the chilling touch with open arms.

It doesn't take long to find the courtyard. It's a beautiful place filled with dark gray stone and rose bushes, wildflower beds, and intricately carved gray stone benches. A previous queen must have requested such gorgeous things. A grand idea that was.

I decide to slow my pace and admire each way the massive plants use their vines to wrap around the open iron gates. There is unique beauty in the way certain flowers bloom under the moon's gentle blue light.

A raw energy of goodness swarms this place. I've never seen anything like it.

The deeper I go into the courtyard the more I can hear running water. Soon I spot a glorious fountain, a big gray stone sculpture of a Madlock king. I can't see which of the kings he is. But it's obvious this is a new addition to this place. Maybe it's Dragoona Madlock.

Crystal-clear liquid spurts out from a tall staff the man held. The smell of clean rainwater wafts into my nose. Inhale the scent and let it calm my racing heart. It sparkles under the small flaming torch I hold toward it. The crown on top of his head is the same as Kasper's. I was right, it is passed down from king to king. Not sure why I suggested that they make new ones for every king.

Seekers, I want to stay here forever and bask in this certain and treasured beauty. But when a set of angry footsteps start to echo all around, I quickly dunk my torch into the fountain to put out the light and hide behind the nearest bush. Jumpy nerves float in my throat.

It's hard to see in this sudden darkness. A gloomy sheen gradually coats the courtyard. Though not enough to make me completely blind to the person who storms inside. A man covered in a lavish black velvet cloak rushes into the courtyard holding a blaring lantern. His face isn't turned to me, but I know it's the warlock Crowlen by the tone of his angry voice.

"I do not care what must be done. Someone other than me used magic. The king does not care about such things. He should. Kasper has to know there hasn't been another wielder of magic other than me for thirty years in this city. Seekers, this is outrageous!" Any louder and he'd be shouting. Waking the sleeping citizens with his loud tone.

I duck down lower as he starts passionately pacing back and forth. His cloak flies behind him, a dark wave of fabric almost blending with his hair.

"His Majesty does not yet understand the gravity of this new situation. It will take some motivation for King Kasper to get into action." I didn't see another man walking inside this secluded place at first.

But once I spot him I can see that he's short enough and a drastic gloomy bushes. Oh, it's the messenger from yesterday! I'll be damned, I can't remember his name. My brows scrunch together as I search my brain to find it.

Crowlen leans down and snarls into the man's unnaturally pale face. "I do not care. No one other than me is allowed to use magic unless it's absolutely needed, which it never is! I will find this danger and deliver her head onto a silver platter."

"How do you know it's a woman? It could be a man from one of the border villages." That smaller man shouldn't have asked such a question.

I freeze as Crowlen stops dead in his tracks. His tall form turns around. The light from the lantern catches his face perfectly. The strong muscles in his jaw tick and that glare he sports is deadly.

"No bitch with the gift of magic is stupid enough to step foot in Thrallen." Oh, Seekers. The look on his face means death for the woman who unwillingly caught his attention.

My heart sinks into my stomach when I realize that woman is me. Fear invades my being as Crowlen snags Coven with his free hand and pulls them both out of the courtyard. Leaving me with shaking knees from keeping bent for so long. Seems like they spent enough time floating around the pretty flowers.

I have this horrible feeling. The attitude Crowlen has over women with magic is just terrible. My old village did not care for such things. There were three other children besides me who could do strange tricks with their minds, the Edderson triplets. Those kids caused too much trouble in Coplina during our early years. Another reason why my father wanted me to keep my power to myself. To hide it away before some got hurt like the Edderson triplets' parents who died in a surprise drowning in a creak outside of Coplina.

Crowlen is a scary man with a surreal face. It is surely best to stay away.

I tuck a stray strand of hair behind my ear and get out from the bush I hid behind. It's best I be on my way to the grounds.

~ ~ ~

The rest of the trip to the training grounds is fast and easy. I encounter no one else. Walking across the open field of green grass is liberating.

Lanterns are scattered around, making it simple to find the weapons Aunty Kurty spoke of. Many shiny sparkling pieces catch my eyes rather suddenly.

After moving to a random patch of luscious grass I drop my bag, it lands with a thud. Then I move to slide out the sword from my thick tunic. It isn't an exactly swift motion, but I retrieved it anyhow.

Perhaps my struggle was because all I have is squishy flesh and little to no muscle built up. That better change soon during my secret practices. My success in the tournaments depends on this.

I remember that there's a cloth in my bag, I take it out to

wipe across the battered blade once and then twice. It now has a nice shine. I'm satisfied enough to leave it and go on searching for what's the priority.

After a few moments, I find the bows and arrows rack. Each bow has been carved from various pieces of wood, no two are the same. I smile at this. No two knights are the same but when they join to fight for a just cause then they are one. Sort of like when an arrow is paired with its bow. I think that is rather fitting for me and the trials.

The wooden shaft and tight string feel oddly comfortable in my hands. I hoist a quiver full of flimsy arrows with a soft tip and frilly yellow feathers at their ends. It takes me a moment to figure out how they are supposed to sit upon my back. Though I manage just fine for a moment.

I approach the target closest to me. It's just a pale-yellow bale of hay that has three red rings painted on it. I'm unsure where to stand before it. Should I step closer in front of the hay or more toward my left? Ugh, this is more frustrating than I originally anticipated.

When it comes down to making sure the arrow stays against the string, I hate it. My hands are so small compared to the grooves on the bow that it's difficult to hold properly. Well, this should be no matter. I inhale the warm late-night air around me and straighten my spine.

During my exhale I pull the arrow to me and let it loose.

Maybe an hour has been spent attempting to launch arrows a mere foot away. I roll up my sleeves and then tuck my hair into the old cap I wore in the signing tent. I have a feeling that this is about to get ugly.

Sweat rolls down my face and gets trapped in my eyelashes. A few drops leak into my eyes. The sting of them forces me to reel back with a hiss.

"I will never get past this!" I cry out furiously.

After a while, I toss down the bow, angrily scatter the leftover arrows, and stomp away. Far enough to where I can openly kick around my cap, chunks of grass flying into the air from my rough feet. Never in my life have I had such explosions of anger like this. This really isn't the time for these pesky emotions to get in the way of my quest.

"What the fuck are you doing?" The voice of an angry Artis shouts behind me, causing me to trip over the cap and land on my knees.

I give a brutal sniff. "Best not to use such words in front of a lady."

That is the only defense I can muster. Not very effective I should guess.

The big man crosses his arms. A furious glint washes over his deadly eyes. Street torches make his shining head glow and that long beard of his darker.

"I'll say whatever the fuck I want, girl. There is no lady in my sight." He only says this to frighten me. But I'm honestly too pissed at myself to care. It's easy to bury his words underneath my own anger.

I struggle to my feet. I dust my pants free of dirt and grass. Though I don't meet his gaze. All I do is pick up the training weapons I treated so horribly. It gives me a slight pain to see the messy feathers of the arrows. I will be more careful with them in the future if I still have one after this night.

"Answer the question, Anna." He snarls, his voice deep and full of irritation. The same sound he always makes. I wonder if he's going to be like this for the rest of my stay.

I slam the bow onto the nearest bench crafted from rich

brown wood and iron screws. "What does it look like I'm doing?"

My sarcasm is very noticeable. It makes Artis scoff.

"Seems to me that you aren't here to only see the Knight Trials. You intend to compete." He does not miss the mark.

That very true accusation causes tears to swell in my eyes and slip down my face. In defeat, I slowly turn around to face him. It almost makes Artis drop his harsh expression. Almost.

"If you must think that I am a fool you are correct. Why would a silly girl in this world want to participate in a sport only meant for men? I'll tell you why." My voice is shaky. Artis only stares and waits for my words.

Good because he is so going to get a mouthful of them from me.

I clean my dripping nose onto my tunic sleeve. I don't care how unladylike it seems.

"Because I am meant to do nothing else. All my life I've wanted to be something spectacular. Becoming a knight of Thrallen is the perfect dream. I am so close to making it happen. It's on the tips of my fingers. I can feel it in here." My hands automatically touch the place in between my breasts. I feel the harsh beating of the blood-pumping organ beneath my ribcage.

I'm not sure whether I mean my soul or heart, perhaps it's both that I know rests my potential.

"The only thing that will cause my failure is the lack of knowledge and this stupid gift that I cannot use." In my boiling anger, I don't catch that I slip and briefly mention magic.

Though Artis instantly catches onto my tragic mistake. He rushes for me and grips my shoulders tightly, shaking me like a bean doll.

"You've got magic?" His face is so close to mine that I cringe away instantly. That foul stench of the mead on his breath wafts into my nostrils.

I want to run away into the woods. To go back home to an empty shack. At least I would be free from this idiotic wish. I may not be cut out for this after all.

"I was born with this power. I was born with magic in my hands." I shakily raise my hands between us. A soft green glow erupts from my fingers, not strong enough to trigger the magic detector spell encasing the city. It's my magic waiting to be let out. It calls to me, I must continue to ignore it. Or else I'll be in so much more trouble.

"Why? Why did you come here? This is not the place for a woman like you here, Anna." His once voice full of savagery slims down into one of terror. Artis can't hide his sorrow for me.

I can't stand the fear in his big dark eyes. It's as if the subject of magic is a dreadful one. Surely men can freely wield their gifts. Why should he be afraid of powers at all?

The big tavern owner releases me. I rub at my now throbbing shoulders. There is no visible trust between him and me. Should I run while I still have the chance?

Why did I open my mouth? Why did he react in such ways?

I speak after a few moments, not wanting to be engulfed in this silence any longer. "I needed to come here. My life will be worth nothing if I don't become a knight. It's my only dream. My magic has nothing to do with the Knight Trials. I promise you that."

The truth lies within my words. I never thought my magic would be involved with the trials. It was never brought up in conversations with my father. I just figured it would soon

81

fizzle out due to my lack of using it, but I know that's not the case anymore.

I don't wait for any more violent words to come out of his mouth. I begin to move around again, gathering every piece of armor I pulled out to try on. There are some parts that are either too small or too big. Nothing fits right on my curved being. It's another obstacle in this apparently impossible path.

But I halt my actions when Artis's shoulders sag greatly. A new leaf has been turned for him within the blink of an eye. I crave to know exactly why this hurts him so much. It doesn't make any sense. Nothing about him makes sense.

It must have something to do with his stubborn age.

"I will help you with the Knight Trials." His softer tone takes me for a spin.

My mouth drops open. If left hanging agape too long, I might catch flies.

"And why should I trust you? Why help someone like me?" I pull one of his moves, acting tough in order to hide these true feelings.

It feels odd to cross my arms in such a serious manner. But this won't stop my growing attitude. I don't think anything will at this point.

Artis seems to change suddenly. I watch him curse under his breath, scratching away at his beard, probably regretting his words. I don't blame him for it either. I wouldn't want to help me all just the same.

"This era is coming to an end. A great war is on its way. Thrallen needs a fierce woman with power. You've got snow hair from a very old line of witches. Pointed ears that signify your hidden lineage that even the Seekers are afraid of. So strong and evil that my childhood village would tell nasty bedtime stories about them. I do not know how you've wandered into this kingdom. But a force of nature like you should aid this battle greatly. The gods above the Seekers have sent you for this very purpose." He finally answers.

His eyes are soft and tender, almost looking like a big brother I never had.

There isn't anything else for me to do but linger in shock with eyes wide and moist. My mouth opens like a suffering fish out of water. The trembling of my shoulders isn't an immediate concern.

I try to come up with anything to say. The source of my silly hair color is unknown. But this man, this Artis, knows more than I ever have in my entire life. I figure instantly that I need to know everything he does.

Though I manage to scrounge up some courage from the legendary pits of the underplace.

"If you really think I can make a difference then be my guest. I want your teaching. I want to become a knight."

The rest of the night goes smoothly. Artis makes me pick up the arrows and bow. His caring mood is now gone completely. Only to be replaced by one of grand focus. He shows me how to stand professionally. How a real knight should present himself. Tells me the perfect distance to be in front of the target.

Of course, I can barely get a handle on holding the arrow straight and steady. But after a few dozen tries I finally get the hang of it.

I feel like a massive heavy boulder once we walk back to the Yellow Piggle. My arms are jelly. The ache within my calves screams away with each step I take. Never have I been so happy to see that brick of a cot when I get back inside my room.

I sleep like a babe after that. Dark images of salty waves and cackling witches fill my dreams.

Twelve

"I don't think this is necessary," I whine as Artis drags me along to the only blacksmith in Celeste Square. An attitude is beginning to form within my being.

I already hate the idea of meeting new people.

Early this morning he banged a fist upon my door, demanding me to hurry and dress. We have a day full of lessons ahead, he said. I don't want to get on his bad side again. My rush to put on a pair of breeches and a worn tunic was a quick one.

Artis scoffs at my ridiculous words. "You can't enter the archery field in borrowed armor." He says as if it's so damn simple.

I don't dare stop the groan that flees from my lips. What a nice day this will be. Saturday just can't get here any faster.

"But won't I just be temporarily using his armor too? I bet you haven't thought of that." In my mind, there is no point to this. My claims seem reasonable enough.

The breastplate, arm cuffs, and shoulder pads I have are enough. But apparently not for this big man. He sure does act like a grandfather. I know better than to say this out loud. So, I stifle a laugh when we approach an open blacksmith shop on Penny Lane, a dandy little street of the city with rougher shops for those who enjoy that sort of thing.

Another big man like Artis hammers down dramatically on a nice bronze sword. Its blade is glowing bright red from the fire. Dark smoke blossoms around him. As if a thousand shadows decide to make their presence known and contort around him.

As we reach the edge of the little shop, he stills his movements and gazes upon Artis who now puffs his chest like a mighty bear. At first, I think this other man wants to poke out Artis's eyes. But then his deadly frown melts into a furious grin.

"Hello, Artis. What brings you by on this fine morning?" He too is covered in dark swirls of ink. Though his beard is brighter in color. Like a silky shade of oak wood. It's braided down to his chest.

They honestly could be brothers for all I know.

The owner of the Yellow Piggle chuckles, a funny noise coming from him. "I've come to cash in my favor, Doniku."

"Ah, I should have known. And who might be that wee babe behind your back?" Doniku is certainly interested in me while

I slightly cower behind the tavern owner. Though I'm not looking forward to being introduced. Too bad I don't have a choice.

However, Artis steps aside and puts me fully on display. I have no idea what to do with my hands, I shove them behind me and instantly pick at the skin around my nails.

I hate you, I mentally curse.

Choosing a route of nobility, I give my own version of a grin where only half of my lips shift upward. The blacksmith doesn't care about my harshness. He sends a grand smirk right back at me.

"I'm Anna Scarrow." I resist the urge to stick out my hand and offer it to him.

"What is it that you ask of me?" Doniku shifts his gaze back to his old friend. I notice that they've known each other for many years. Something I couldn't relate to. I have no friends of my own.

Artis sighs whilst looking around. I already detest having such big secrets. Now my new mentor must hide some of his as well that aren't even his to keep. I can't tell if my father would be disappointed or not.

The large man with a bald head then voices his demands. "I need a full set of armor to fit this girl." He points a chubby finger at me.

I may be fuming on the inside, but I ignore the burning to nod my head anyway.

Doniku stalks towards me like a lion, his large dark green eyes piercing my soul almost. I fight the desire to crouch in a protective way. It puzzles me as to why he studies every inch of my short frame. Probably mentally measuring me. That is a rather handy skill to have in this profession of his.

Suddenly he backs away. "I'll do it."

That was that.

He does in fact write down the numbered lengths of my legs, arms, back, and chest. But when it comes down to my head, I laugh terribly. The oddest thing is to have a head sized for a helmet.

I giggle occasionally as a long string is wrapped around my neck and forehead. It's ticklish indeed as the tips of his fingers feather across my skin. I must appear ridiculous to any passing folks who peer into the shop.

Before long me and Artis return after he has a private conversation with the blacksmith. I don't want to eavesdrop. So, scanning my eyes upon the close people of Thrallen is a good option. It gives me a chance to engrave the everyday lives of these people into my mind. One day soon I'll be one of the knights to protect them. None of them know it yet.

~ ~ ~

"We have four more nights to prepare you. I expect great improvement. If not, you will surely miss the target." Artis doesn't hold back his dreadful doubts as we leave for the Yellow Piggle. I'm doing my best to keep up with his long strides. I don't like his piss-poor attitude about it all.

"You have so little faith." I point out the obvious.

All he does is grunt for an answer. Pressing for more words from him won't do any good. I can only walk by his side, glancing over the town, taking in every hut and shop, noting where secluded places are located.

My mind is a distant object after that short hour in the blacksmith shop. I don't speak up to ask any other questions.

I keep to myself most of the time. If there is a need to speak, I'll keep it for the training.

It's clear that Kurty has begun to worry about me. I give her my best smile whenever I can find one within me. Still, I don't think it's enough to convince her that I'm alright. But at least I'm getting somewhere during the nights spent in the training grounds.

I'm still surprised she has no idea what we are doing or goes out of her way to question why I've been back to the tavern late covered in aches.

I do actually start shooting the arrows in the proper way. I just can't seem to aim worth a shit. And yet when I inhale deeply and close one eye and release my arrow it strikes true at the center. So, it is possible for me to do this.

No one knows the specific requirements for the trial. I'm not sure what counts as a win. However, word has spread that the competitors will be assigned a shooting group. At least I won't be alone during this first trial.

~ ~ ~

"Take it easy tomorrow. You've earned a break." Artis tells me on this bland Thursday night. There are no stars that are out to guide me in the right direction. Not even the warm winds have come blowing in support.

We have barely finished position drills for quick shots. My entire back and shoulder blades are on fire. Heavy sweat lathers my hair. A shaky tremble takes over my short arms.

I lower the bow. I could be mistaken as a skilled hunter if it wasn't for my face of pure exhaustion.

"Thank you." I exhale.

I don't waste time bathing underneath warm water after rushing back to the Yellow Piggle and all its warm and cozy glory. Aunty Kurty has this big old horse barrel waiting for me back at the tavern. The soapy liquid smells of freshly cut grass and lemon. I'm very much in the heavens as soon as my feet are submerged.

It's been three solid hours of me soaking beneath the water and I don't give a damn. The water going cold is no bother. I welcome the coolness to wrap around my bruised body, letting the lathering liquid consume my constant fears of the upcoming trial.

There is nothing else on my mind. I constantly must reel myself back into reality and not be tortured by whatever future awaits me.

I take my sweet time getting ready for bed. I gently rake through my wet hair with a brush Aunty Kurty gifted me yesterday morning. It feels wonderful to glide my hands through the damp white locks.

Tonight, after sinking underneath my blankets, I peer out the window, watching bats swoop underneath the lights sprayed out by the lanterns. A sour taste sits on my tongue all the time now. However, on this night it's stronger. The warlock Crowlen is near, but why?

My eyes are so close to falling shut when a loud bang shoots through the tavern. I'm quick to my feet. I gather my nightgown's skirt in hand before racing down the stairs to find Aunty Kurty holding a frying pan and Artis carrying an axe.

I suddenly feel out of place, never having experienced such things before. But I push the thought of being exposed to the side and join the older couple. I'll fight against whatever in any way I can.

Artis stands tall and does not let his voice falter. "Who goes there?"

I catch a chill from his stone-like speech. Kurty brings me close by the elbow. I take this as a chance to slowly shift behind them, waiting to see what dangers welcome us in the dead of night.

"Good night, dear tavern owner. The warlock of King Kasper requests a visit of your house." Crowlen barks from the other side of the door.

Panic then floods into my body like rushing river water. A striking chill enters my chest. Aunty Kurty notices me fidgeting with the sleeves of my nightgown.

"Stay calm, Anna." She whispers into my ear whilst gently swatting my hand away.

I attempt to give her a small smile, but it comes out as a grimace instead.

"What the hell for?" Artis shouts back. His chest rises and falls madly.

I don't understand how Artis can ever so clearly disrespect such a powerful man. I keep my mouth shut as Kurty jerks me back when the door flings open with no true warning.

My quickly beating heart drops to the floor as my eyes fuse with Crowlen's. The red shine of them causes me to shiver involuntarily. My body convulses slightly. His pale skin glows white from the lantern he holds up high. His fierce face bites back an annoyed growl. It's unsettling how much I find him attractive at this moment.

I gulp nervously.

"Should have known a bitch like you would hide out in a dump like this." He seethes in my direction.

I believe I piss myself a little from fear and odd attraction for this man colliding within me. Seekers, what's wrong with me?

He storms into the house with a massive deep blue cape flowing behind him. His raven hair whips around in all our faces. It smells of smoke from a bonfire and a strange sweetness from some sort of berry. I'm going mad.

I bother not to take his words into any serious consideration. I refuse to let him get to me. However, the tavern owner shoots me an accusing glare, silently telling me to keep quiet. Obviously, I ignore it for now.

Artis appears rather panicky himself. I tilt my head to try and dig the reason out of him. But he quickly shakes his head. As if telling me to lay low and not draw attention to myself.

Easier said and done because now I know exactly why this monster of a magic wielder is here ransacking houses. Crowlen is hunting for witches. He's hunting me.

Crowlen searches behind the bar. Then a few castle guards march inside after him. They go ahead and snoop around trying to find something useful or someone to arrest.

They are supposed to be looking for an illegal witch. And that dear witch happens to be me. I'm fucked. So damn fucked.

"What is the meaning of this?" Kurty doesn't attempt to hide her ferocious tone.

I watch the much older woman wave around the pan. I then wish for such energy. That is the confidence and brutal passion I need for Saturday. Maybe I can somehow borrow some of it.

Crowlen slams an empty mug onto the counter, making the dishes and cups shake from the strong force he used.

He sneers in a sinister tone. "I'm looking for a woman with

magic. Haven't seen one of those, have you, Artis?"

My entire body is on high alert. My palms begin to sweat. A nervous chatter of my teeth wants to echo out into the air. Is this my magic acting up? No, please, not now!

I'm smart enough to not look over to my mentor. That would surely give me away. I must stand up tall like Artis and act like nothing is the matter with me. Because there isn't. I'm completely fine.

"You aren't going to find one of those here," Artis says this like a woman who possesses magic is worth nothing. His nasty words make me grow cold.

Then I fight an internal battle. I obviously know Artis really doesn't feel that way. If he did then I would have been arrested and killed days ago. But it still hurts to hear that from him.

They are only for the warlock.

The man with wild hair stops his frantic pacing for a moment. I find myself subtly admiring the way his lean muscular thighs flex beneath his leather breeches. Perhaps I'm finding amusement in watching his angry face crease with frustration.

Just as quickly as those silly thoughts appear, they vanish when Crowlen gets a little too close for comfort.

"I shall be the judge of that." The way he snarls into Artis's face which urges me to slap him around a few times. That bubbling anger within my chest wants to burst open and wield him to rot from the inside out.

But as the taste of spice begins to flood my mouth, I hurry to pack all those negative feelings back in.

Don't let it out. Keep yourself calm. My father's words are an unexpected source of positivity. Words that I will take to my grave.

For I am glad it is only a sliver of my magic to rumble. Crowlen would waste no time in binding my hands and taking me to the king if he truly tasted it himself. Good thing he is too wrapped up in arguing with Artis. Kurty jumps in a few times with her own rash comments.

I stand back and just hold myself, crossing my arms around me tight. There really isn't much for me to do. Eventually, I take a seat at the nearest table.

After a while, Crowlen and his guards leave but not before shooting me, who's almost asleep, with a look of disgust.

It results in me feeling somewhat sad. Annoyed even.

Why does he seem to hate me so much? I question myself when Artis and his wife sit down beside me, their expressions grim.

Artis sighs, his forehead creasing deeply, and putting his head into his hands. A tremble of anger shakes his body. Kurty gently pats his shoulder. Guilt threatens to take me over. If I hadn't used my magic my first day here, then Thrallen wouldn't have called upon its warlock for a witch hunt. Wait, does this mean King Kasper has formed the Witch Findings again? Heck, I may be from Delvina but I'm sure a lot of people have been told about the brutal hunts from almost thirty years ago.

There hasn't been a search like that anywhere for decades. And now I seemed to have started them up again. All just for me to catch a glimpse at the hunter himself. I'm a damn fool.

"This is all my fault. Crowlen will stop at nothing till he catches and kills me." I say in tears to Artis. Kurty stares out in surprise.

"What do you mean?" She asks. Curiosity is not what fuels her words, only pure terror.

I do nothing but look at her with such self-loathing swimming in my belly. "I'm the woman he's come to look for. He wouldn't have raided this kingdom if I hadn't used magic those few days ago."

Kurty's eyes grow wide and watery. I feel the disappointment seep out from the woman and flow in waves.

Silence consumes the empty pub. Not even music from a cricket echoes. Just the sounds of heavy breathing.

"Why is it that you are here? Where do you and Artis go at the break of the night?" Kurty is oblivious to our plan.

It makes me feel all the more horrible about it. Before I open my mouth to speak Artis beats me to it.

"I've been training her for the Knight Trials. She has illegal magic. And I won't stop until she has fulfilled her life's dream. You can be mad all you want. This is my redemption." His last words confuse me. Though I keep my head down and say nothing.

Kurty seems to understand what he means, and she too doesn't have the guts to oppose his wish.

All three of us go back to our beds. I barely sleep till the first morning light shines into the window.

Thirteen

Crowlen

I never wanted to hit something so bad in my entire life like I do right now.

Having that girl watch me like a hawk was irritating beyond belief. I don't know how I can still manage to stomach the feeling of her intense eyes on me. It was truly eerie.

Sparks of rage spill out of me. Nothing is supposed to get past me in Thrallen. And yet I can't pinpoint the location of that terribly potent magic. It's such an intoxicating flavor of juicy cinnamon. I can't ever forget such scents that sprawled into the air.

It appeared at that moment for a reason. Perhaps a task presented by the Seekers to test me and my power. It wouldn't pass them.

Somehow, someway, I know Anna has something to do with all of this bullshit. Though I don't understand the why of it.

Those hazel eyes of hers cause a brutal storm of chaos to brew within me.

Why did she have to show up for the trials? Too many questions and absolutely no answers in my line of red sight.

Once again, I pace around my bedchamber like a brooding crow, my namesake. The creatures that influence trouble when they should not. Whoever gave me the name of course knew what they were doing.

I speak into the room to get a better grasp of this, firing off questions, not expecting anyone to answer. A thing I do to calm the racing power that thrums in my veins.

I will not allow my mind and body to properly rest till this witch is burned on a stake in Celeste Square or drowned in the southern river that is hidden in a patch of oak trees. I shall rejoice in her glorious suffering. The tendrils of my magic crave the taste of her blood. Oh, it shall be a glorious triumphant day indeed.

But when I accidentally utter Anna's name in my own personal space, I stop moving entirely. Blood rushes throughout my muscles and bones like a forest fire. Feelings twist in my guts from sudden ideas.

It's as if a lantern is blazing inside my mind. A nasty grin graces my thin lips. The red glow of my eyes brightens the room, casting shadows of the many bottled potions and cauldrons I have littering every available space. I am a roaring candle in the night. A wicked flame begging to sizzle flesh.

Anna must know where the witch is. She can be hiding her for all I know. There's no other explanation. I will stop at nothing till I rip the truth right from her pretty pale throat.

Fourteen

S aturday rolls in on a blazing arrow right into my heart. Horrid emotions stir within me. Artis arrived at the blacksmith's shop to retrieve my custom armor early this morning. I really feel reality slam into me once spotting each piece sitting on the bar when I come down for breakfast.

Aunty Kurty made sure I appeared like a proper man. She bothers to pull out fancy body paints and carefully draws a beard on my face. And gives my hair a little toss around. Artis pitches in to aid his wife with creating my hair into a mop of sorts. It takes the longest to tie back the short strands with a leather strap. Small pieces keep falling around my eyes. Kurty groans and just leaves it all be.

This time I don't bother to stuff a pillow up my shirt. The breastplate should be enough of a disguise. It's already perfectly tough and thick to help the illusion of me having a man's form. I'm sure Artis was the one to tell the blacksmith to make no special accommodation for it, meaning there is a wall of six abdominal muscles going down my front.

All day yesterday Kurty told me what is to be expected. Turns out Artis also had stopped by the blacksmith to request a noble seal to be carved into my shield. My jaw dropped in awe as I took in a massive lion head gracing the metal. It's a total surprise to me.

I pretend I can hear its mighty roar. They have done good work to make me a true noble. I hope that it's enough to keep me through the trials.

~ ~ ~

Me and the other competitors arrive at the contest field rather early, four hours early to be exact. It appears I'm not the only one with such an idea. It gives us the time to practice our stances and aim before entering the arena.

Dread pools in my belly. Maybe I'm not mentally prepared for this. I want to be. But this is more than I anticipated.

Looking at all these fierce men waiting to show off their skills is terrifying. I glance at all of them, closely watching the way their arms rise when posing for ladies who walk by. Their flirty smirks make my guts roll.

Hordes of armor-covered men stand tall with bows and arrows in hand. They rise like castle towers. Their height is easily intimidating. I'm a mushroom compared to these beasts. I don't stand a chance in hand-to-hand combat. The knighthood better train me for that when the time comes. If it ever does.

Artis leaves his wife and me to find the starting times and groups. He quickly comes back after an hour with a smile on his face. "You're with the first group. You'll be called upon by the horn. Don't worry too much about it. Just hit the target three times and you'll continue to the next trial." He's so confident in his words.

So badly I want to believe in his enthusiasm. However, the nerves in me try their best to stun me, they attack me as if they were rabid dogs. I'd much prefer a crow to peck out my eyes.

Instead of bursting into tears, I nod back in understanding. Sudden paranoia starts to eat at my spirit. Like there are thousands of people staring right into my soul.

But as the hours pass more and more townspeople fill the massive arena stands like a colony of ants moving up the trunk of a tree. I can hear their stomps from here. The stands are so tall in the sky that they create walls around the dirt field in the middle.

After a few minutes of standing there with sweat trailing down my back, the crowd inside goes man. Their cries and splendid shouts fill my ears to the brim. King Kasper must have just entered the arena.

I'm going to puke before I even make it inside. The need to evict my breakfast which consisted of wild black berries and oats hangs within me. It's a daily meal that I've grown fond of. I wonder if my face is turning green. I sure do feel hot like a flame. When did spring become so hot?

Kurty shifts her eyes to me, they burn the side of my face

almost. "Do not look anywhere else but your target. Once everyone is done shooting their arrows the judges will come out to score. Those who've passed the trial will be asked to step out off the field. All you must do is hit the target. Make every shot count. Please."

I stand there with tears in my eyes. Those words are everything I needed to hear. It almost feels as if I'm being mothered. And that's the best thing in the world right now. Before I can thank her the silence that once engulfs the trial participants quickly dissolves.

A horn goes off with a thunderous blast. This is it. There is no turning back from this. It's my destiny.

Me and nine other men march into a perfectly straight line, our armor clinking in sync. My heart stops for a moment. I can see Artis holding onto Kurty's hand tightly. That gives me all the motivation I need.

I'm left at the very end of the formation. Taking my helm from under my arm I place it on my head along with the others. Some of my hearing is muted but I doubt that will be for long.

The rushing of my blood almost consumes any thoughts or feelings I have.

We move forward with the intention of making it out of the trial triumphant. There is a lanky man toward the front who leads us into the side opening and onto the arena ground. Then we follow behind and one by one stop in front of our targets. We're a row of playing bricks. All we have to do now is wait till someone knocks us over.

The crowd of citizens of graceful Thrallen roar as King Kasper rises from a simple throne carved from the wood that litters the forest around the big wall encasing the city. Strong shouts make my head groan.

He wears beautiful robes again, only this time the color of fresh rain and pale green. The king waves to us all while simultaneously silencing his people with a stern gaze. The thumping of my own heart is all the sound that calls to me. Its thrashing beat keeps me steady.

"Great people of Thrallen, I welcome you to the Knight Trials. On this evening, we will test three hundred men on their archery skills and see who passes onto the next trial." His voice is pure and proud. He speaks to each one of us it seems.

I gaze at the crowd, studying how they watch him intently. But then my eyes snag on the warlock standing to his left. Suddenly, my mood sours tenfold. He's still brooding and extremely agitated. I can tell by the way he taps his fingers against his leather breeches. I'd be surprised if he doesn't run off during the first group out of boredom.

Oh, Seekers, he looks even more delectable today than he did in the market. I tell myself to take deep breaths.

His robes are of a similar style to the king's. The only big difference is the color. Dark purple velvet wraps around his body like a glove of fear. The thread trim is a rich red tone, perhaps meant to appear as blood. It seems he has a signature theme. I should say it fits him rather well. Hatred for how much I'm paying attention to him pulls me out of my thoughts and back to the king.

Kasper smiles brightly at all of us. At this moment I feel a part of Thrallen. It's an emotion I never want to let go of or give away to someone who doesn't deserve it.

Big things are about to happen.

He peers with those stormy ocean eyes. "You, my brave people, have chosen to participate in a wondrous task. Please, do be careful, for the arrow is sharp and bowstring tight. When

103

the horn blows you will have three chances to hit the target. Don't waste the shots."

Kasper sits back down on his large brown portable throne. He does it in such a way that expels grace and humility. Yes, I hope to serve in his army of knights someday soon.

I turn my line of sight to the painted haybale before me. A bright red-ringed target facing me like a raging bull during mating season. I attempt to steady my breathing. Each breath I take in and out is quickly forgotten as I feel the heated vision of Crowlen upon me. Not even the thunderous crowd can distract me.

Once the horn blasts away I know not to get all flustered. Artis would surely scold me for messing up due to a shaky form. It's not hard to imagine the painful expression he is very capable of making.

With another smooth motion, I retrieve a single arrow from my borrowed quiver made of soft brown leather with gold bears painted on the sides. I hear the others gradually release the pointed sticks into the air. However, I take my time in aligning the arrow against the taut string.

I spy a preferable area to shoot the arrow. After a few moments of positioning my feet, I thrash my first arrow before me. I feel the end-feather graze my cheek in a hurry, it takes my breath away, making my heart stop. It's as if time becomes still around me. My jaw drops underneath my helm as I intensely observe the way the faint wind carries the sharp point of it forward. Tears spring to my eyes after it lands right on the outer ring.

Screams of joy flood my throat. I've been struggling with even piercing the target during practice. It's a miracle I managed to hit it on the first shot.

I keep cool and collected while fetching another thin arrow.

I don't wait so long to release this one due to the overwhelming confidence that's decided to envelope me. This time the world doesn't stop, and the arrow hits the next inner ring with a true punch.

Meaning I hit another ring. A few warm tears stream down my face. I'm glad my helmet blocks my red face from view. I don't want anyone to see the river of excited snot going past my lips. It's all a temporary break from my reality. I need to pull myself back into the now and get this finished before I lose my nerve.

With a moment to spare, I glance down the line at my other competitors. Me and a few others remain. I hadn't noticed others were quickly shown out of the arena. Better luck next time.

Many arrows are sticking out of the dirt. I don't give myself the chance to feel bad for the one who didn't succeed. In fact, I shall dedicate my very possible win to them. They are in my thoughts, for now.

There's one more arrow that needs to be aimed.

My shaking fingers clumsily grip the final arrow in the quiver, sweat dampens my palms. Even after adjusting my knees, the shakes are still rampaging through me. I must do this either way. My only option is to ignore my sudden nerves and get on with it.

The arrow keeps swaying away from the string. A few lines of curse words slip out from my lips. A shout of anger waits in my mouth, clawing against the back of my teeth to be set free. Lashing out in a fit of rage isn't worth it.

I swallow a massive breath and let my instinct flow right into my hands. The magic in me feels the arrow slowly lay against the bowstring. My lungs steadily inflate and release a breath now filled with calm energy I didn't know I possessed.

There is something inside of me that wants me to pause my hasty desire to be the best. All I need to do is perform true to my abilities.

Hesitantly, I let my eyes flutter shut. That familiar touch of the end-feather caresses the side of my mouth once the arrow is set in motion.

My ears pick up no sounds of this mighty arrow of mine sticking into the dry ground. I open one eye to find where it did manage to land. Something inside me breaks. My magic swirls in the pit of my belly.

Right there in the center of this magnificent target lies my mystical arrow. More tears rain down my face. I actually did it. I've made it to the next trial! Oh, my Seekers, this is really happening, isn't it?

The horn blows again and rips me from my inner delight. Three men dressed in yellow pants and brown coats make their way onto the field. They each start walking towards us at different sections of the line. One man with terrible yellow hair approaches me and I give him my best smile even though he can't see it. He leans down to peer at my target with a careless glint in his muddy eyes.

"Name?" He asks me.

"Mason Triscan, sir." I answer in a deep tone. Hopefully, he doesn't notice the feminine way my dirty hands dangle at my sides.

He lifts and peers down at my rigid form. A wide smile blossoms on his lips. "Congratulations. Mason Triscan, you have earned your place in the next trial. Please, go out the way you came."

Is it possible for my heart to burst from joy? I sure as fuck hope not!

I give a courtesy bow towards the king who doesn't bother to glance in my direction before walking away. Pure shock laces my thick bones. It feels unreal to even be in Thrallen right now.

This means I get to join the jousting trial next week. This is the best moment of my life. What happened?

The moment I'm free of the arena I gasp roughly and tear off my helmet. The air is warm, offering a now more forceful breeze. It guides me away from the king and the crowd and Knight Trial competitors.

Waiting for me in Celeste Square are the tavern owner and his splendid wife. Worried expressions they sport. But once their eyes land on me they turn hysterical. Great joy breaks across their wilted features with ease.

"What happened?" Kurty asks her in a serious tone. She grabs my face and inspects me for any possible injuries.

"Did you hit the target?" Artis questions me as he smooths back my messy hair, getting it away from my eyes. I'm not surprised it completely fell out of the leather tie.

I wait until they stop fussing over me to say a word. In all honesty, I do not mind their caring ways. It's new for me just as much as it is for them. I will not deny Kurty this.

The smile that forms on my lips is rather sinister, I should say. I wish Crowlen was here to see it. And I wish to see what his reaction would be.

"I think I need to learn how to ride a horse."

Fifteen

J ousting is something of a dream for me.

Never in my life did I think I would ride a horse. Especially one with an attitude such as dear Sarah. A young horse with a tendency to buck me any chance she gets. She neighs at me like a wild man, ready to rip my head clean off my shoulders.

I won't be surprised if she suddenly grows fangs and sucks the blood from my neck. Her grim stare is always upon me. I hate horses. With passion.

They take up too much space, can never follow simple

directions, and have those pesky attitudes!

I really struggle to stay on this merciless beast. Groans of my anger heavily fill the air around me. It doesn't dissipate when Artis shoves a lance in my aching hands, hurting from jerking on the reins. A sickening feeling scrawls over my inner stomach lining, curdling with the acid within me.

I have been told to practice prancing around while holding the overly large stick within an armor-gloved hand. Being able to keep it hoisted in the air is a hard enough challenge. Keeping the damned thing straight in the air is so much worse.

Everything is starting to go south fast. I have to get a grip on my sanity before I lose it.

It only takes five days for me to firmly hit the target Kurty made. She crafted it from a mead barrel lid. She is quite clever. Kurty is the one to approach me with the target whenever I ride on the horse with my lance drawn tight. At the very last second of my final training, I strike the target and almost break it in half. Now all I can do is hope it will be enough.

Tomorrow is already the second trial. And yet I still am having trouble thinking that all of this is real. Nothing seems to soothe my ill thoughts about possible failure or worse, being caught by Crowlen. He still lingers about on almost every street corner I turn to. His deadly red gaze seems to follow me any chance he gets. It's like he's been watching me on purpose. I've made a not-so-hesitant choice to rarely leave the tavern unless to train. The less the warlock sees of me the better I shall be

Most nights I stay awake thinking of my father. He's the only thought I have once collapsing onto the hard bed after a rough night of training.

He would have cheered me on brightly if he was here to

see. I only wish he is watching me in the heavens. Maybe my mother is by his side.

The idea brings a sliver of comfort mixed with pain to my dreary soul.

"You've been rather quiet. What's on your mind?" Kurty wonders out loud as I continue munching on a roasted turkey leg.

I don't give a shit about the stares I receive from the tavern regulars. It's only me and the turkey at this moment. My roguish bites are mine alone. Screw everyone else.

"Anna?" Kurty calls me again.

I pause midchew and raise a split brow. Yesterday morning I slipped down the tavern stairs and hit my head. Now I'll always have a faint scar where a rusted nail sliced my flesh.

There is no point in hiding a glare from her. All this preparing for the trials has made me hungry like a bear. She's interrupting very important business of mine, with the turkey leg.

Aunty Kurty shakes her head. "What's been getting you down?"

Oh, she noticed that? Huh.

I set down my still warm unfinished leg back onto the silver plate, carefully wiping my face clean of juices with a brown cloth napkin.

"I just think I got lucky with the first trial. I don't have high hopes for the joust." I speak the bitter truth that continues to linger at the very front of my mind. There is no point in hiding it.

Kurty doesn't seem to like my answer. She gives a throaty laugh that's filled with utter disbelief.

The older woman shoots to her feet. There is an angry glint

in her eyes that I have not seen since the warlock stormed into the tavern a few nights ago.

"The tavern is now closed. Get out!" Kurty cups her hands around her mouth to elongate her furious shout. I even feel her rage within my own bones. I'm in for it now.

A few men groan before exiting the pub somewhat sad that their fun is over. However, not before leaving their required coin on the little table next to the door. At least these withered men have some sense to pay their dues.

Kurty places her chubby hands on her thick womanly hips.

"You better get that sad thinking out of your head before tomorrow. Your group sets the bar for the rest. We can't have you dropping out." Her attempt at being motivational isn't really helping me feel better. It does nothing.

"Did you see that daft horse throw me tonight? I'm a joke. A terrible joke that doesn't belong within Thrallen." Without much reasoning, I jump to my throbbing feet and give my shout loud and clear.

Something inside of my heart must have broken. Emotions I don't want to feel start to drip out of me. Staining the cozy air and turning it almost impossibly foul.

As if an already cracked dam has withered so much that it all comes down to cause a massive wave. Something I am not prepared to talk about. Not with Aunty Kurty. Not with anyone in this world.

I can't stop my hands from flinging around me. "There is no guarantee that I can actually pull off some miracle that I'll succeed in the next trial. All I can think about is failing. Or believing that this really has been a stupid mistake. That my father's wish is for nothing. He must be laughing at me in the heavens now."

Words keep tumbling out of me. I can't stop it. I don't want to feel like this anymore.

All Kurty can do is stand there watching me cry horribly. She waits until I sit back down in a huff. A steady trail of salty tears flows down my flushed face. More threatens to burst from me.

The reality is that I can't help myself. I need to let go of these awful feelings. Never could I have guessed this journey would make me feel so empty and drained. Instant regret fills my guts and slowly climbs into my throat.

I lift my puffy eyes to find Artis now standing beside his wife. Even more dread surfaces in my heart.

"I have never met a girl like you. So strong and hardheaded." Aunty Kurty starts to speak.

A curt scoff escapes me. I roll my eyes.

Artis then raises his hand, letting me know he has something to say. Now I'm more terrified than ever.

"Never has a woman wanted to become a knight. Some might have dreamed once or twice of it. But you are truly halfway there. Soon you shall be training with companies. Getting ready for future battles. Preparing to protect the king at all costs. No one has gotten this far as you have. A woman faking her way into the Knight Trials is already a risk. You have magic, Anna. You are different. No one will ever be as strong as you." Artis's voice cracks.

I caused him and Kurty pain. The last thing I ever wanted to do was hurt them like this. These people mean the world to me. Why haven't I shown them that?

I engraved his carefully thought-out words on the surface of my heart, taking in his proud expression, and I watch his thick eyebrows sink in frustration.

I'm beginning to admire this brutal man who owns the Yellow Piggle.

These people truly care for me and all I do is grip about what I'm not doing right. I haven't stopped for one second to be thankful for all that they've done for me.

Embarrassment consumes me. I sit there in weak silence.

With one strong inhale I raise myself up. I can't stop myself from stumbling about slightly. It doesn't matter how I look at them. I just want to make sure they understand how grateful I am for all of it.

I clear my throat roughly. Their attention is still right on me. I feel small and helpless under their intense gaze.

"I'm sorry. I've never been good with emotion before. I didn't grow up with a mother to show me how to handle womanly things. No one to teach me how to treat a monthly bleed. My father was all I had. And yet I can't seem to believe in myself like he did. You both see all the potential in me that I thought was not possible. I not only need to try harder in my training, but I must start telling myself I can do this." My words are shaky.

I don't wish for them to be more upset. But as I notice Aunty Kurty's tears, I know I have done something stupid. No, I must have said the right thing.

"Thank you both. I shall see you both in the morning." I bow slightly and turn, walking up the steps at a slow agonizing pace, careful not to trip again.

Even preparing for bed is exhausting in the worst way imaginable.

It's a shock that I manage to find any sleep at all after sinking beneath the sheets.

Sixteen

"Y"ou must be strong, girl." Artis pats me on the back roughly. My shoulders jerk forward from the amount of force he of course willingly used. I'm beginning to think he likes to mess with me on purpose.

"What else is there to do?" I ask with a sarcastic tone. Even give a little roll of my eyes.

All he gives me is a shake of his head.

I chuckle, finding his strange enthusiasm comforting.

I feel a lot better than the night before. Though a throbbing ache lingers at the front of my skull. The aftermath of my screaming match still hovers around. Not the best sleep I've had since being in Thrallen.

"I'll lead you and the horse out there and guide you both through the match. You have two chances to knock your opponent off his horse. If you decide to get injured a physician's volunteer will aid you after. Don't you dare fall off." Artis tells me carefully.

Kurty gives her own demands too. Of course, she would have to say something.

I don't expect anything less.

A smile forms on my lips before giving Kurty a discreet hug, making sure no armored men grow suspicious.

My deep inhale of the air around me offers a calm to wash over my nervousness. Me and another nobleman named Carlin Wester will be pitted against each other within the arena. Three other matches have gone before us. We are to be next.

I've seen him standing a little way to our left with his potential squire who holds his dark wood lance. From what I can tell he's massively tall and that pitch black hair of his makes him even more terrifying. He's got a wicked scowl on his face. This man means war.

Before I can turn towards Artis to give him thanks the horn from the last trial blasts into the air. It is now my turn to hopefully beat Carlin.

"Best be off then. Do us proud." Artis says whilst guiding the horse down into the changed arena with me on it.

I was rather sad to know we weren't allowed to ride on our practice horses. So, this beast I'm sitting upon is a stranger to me. I miss that asshole, Sarah.

The hay targets that once were in a line no longer reside

down on the dirt grounds. Instead, a long blockade of some kind cuts the ground in half. My opponent marches down the opposite direction, his shoulders too rigid.

Suddenly, I feel ill. Of course, I don't say a word about this. There is no need for me to lose whatever backbone I have.

"When the horn blows again you better race. Good luck, Anna." Artis gives my armored knee a gentle squeeze before occupying me corner of the arena ground. There he will wait for my return after the second run.

The tavern owner nods to a small stable boy with pale hair. The little fellow dressed in a brown and yellow uniform does his best to walk straight when handing me a lance I'm supposed to use. It's too heavy in my hands. I barely manage to grip it through my leather glove.

I watch Carlin hold his own lance. It seems to fit him better. My eyes latch onto the solid iron ball at its tip. A shudder enters my belly. Are our lances allowed to have special things done to them?

After shaking the uneasy feelings settling in my gut, I roll my shoulders back and pop my neck. This is it. I'm halfway through the trials and still am somehow alive. I know why that is. I need to give myself more credit. My ability to continue fighting proves that my worthless skills aren't too bad after all.

"Thanks," I tell the younger boy. My voice is the right amount of gruff. All he does is bow before me and scurry off with the other children whose families have volunteered to aid the trials.

A few more long moments fly by. I watch Carlin. My eyes are of a serpent. Quick to spot odd aspects of my view.

And then the horn blares again. I instantly kick the sides of my horse to encourage it to gallop ahead at full speed. Carlin is on his path towards me. I can see his sneer even through the small opening of his helm.

I do my best to match it.

Both of our lances are aimed at each chest. The whole world around me slows down, almost to a halt. We're going so fast that I barely manage to register what's happening. That's until a sharp searing pain covers my left side and suddenly my ribs are on fire.

Our horses stop at the other side in full-on pants, their breaths are a small fog in the air despite the warm weather. I feel something warm trickle down my leg.

"What the fuck?" My words shake. I peer down at the piece of my tunic poking out from under my breastplate that is quickly being soaked in my own blood. Dark red fills my vision. I feel faint. There is something sharp sticking out of me. What the fuck?

With shaking fingers, I try nudging it. It jerks within my flesh and causes me to curse. No one hears this over the roaring crowd. They are enjoying this more than I am. Well, at least someone is having fun.

My eyes lift to find Carlin prancing around with his lance high in the air. The people love his energy and confidence. I would have to if it were not for spying on the tip of his weapon. No longer does that odd sphere sit atop it. It's been somehow replaced by a sharp blade. A broken dagger.

He's cheated! The realization sends a wave of anger through me. Or maybe it's my sudden blood loss getting the best of me.

"You're hurt!" Another stable boy approaches me with wide green eyes. His mouth hangs open in panic.

I hurriedly shake my head. "I'm alright, young one."

"Ah, what a thrill! Another go is in order." Kasper shouts in a cheery tone.

Well, who am I to deny the king what he desires?

I adjust on the horse for the final time. My lance doing its best to slip from my hands, sweat filling my glove. My head aches. Everything is going dark. No, I must stay awake.

Carlin shoots forward as the horn goes off again. My body lurches as my horse does the same. At this point, I have no control over this beast.

But I use everything in me to pin the end of the lance to my uninjured side and point it ahead.

I don't fully recognize that my terrifying stick strikes the opposite rider square in the chest until I feel his own hit me again. The wooden pole collides with the center of my breastplate. Its sharp point fails to cause any more damage. The punch is so strong I almost go backward. Though he's the one to topple over and land right into the dark brown dirt.

I silently thank the Seekers for giving my hand a firm grip on the saddle.

It all happened so fast. It doesn't feel real.

The crowds go wild. Their roars shake my eardrums. Me and this damn horse reach the other side where we first started. Artis tries to go up to me but is quickly whisked away out of the arena. Right, they have more matches after me.

A woman with long golden hair, and green eyes, wearing a pink dress now stands in his place waiting for me, her feet taping away.

"You must remove your helmet and claim victory." She tells me. I open my mouth to begin a rather foul protest but hurry to decide against it. It is expected of the victor to prance around for a moment with his helm raised in the air. Stupid rules these all are.

I rip the silver helmet off my boiling head. Steam rises from my scalp, but I don't care. I'm glad my hair remained brought back. I can't tell if the fake beard is properly set anymore. I haven't had the chance to check.

The mystery girl is already shoving my horse back out onto the field.

Once the people spot me, they cheer like mad cows. A very ridiculous smile rises on my lips. I look up to find the king clapping with a wondrous grin. To my surprise, the warlock is giving his own clap as well.

I don't keep eye contact for long for fear that they will recognize me. That warlock is too smart to not sniff out my mask and hang me for treason.

This is the time where I take my helmet and shove it into the air like the knights in all those stories. I'm pleasantly surprised to hear the people go nuts in the stands. Making me almost forget that I'm quickly bleeding out all over the horse.

"Our winner, Mason Triscan!" King Kasper announces it officially to the crowd. I think my eardrums are going to bust. The feelings are very welcome at this moment.

All the excitement dies down once I come back to the corner. A massive throbbing now taking over her chest and side. I think I need rest. It's so hard to breathe. I hope that my lung isn't collapsing.

The woman from earlier helps me off the horse. She drags me out to a row of beige tents lining the arena walls. Her hands clutch me tightly. I grit my teeth from her harsh grip. I can feel more of my blood pour over her hands staining her slightly tan flesh.

"What are you going to do?" I ask rudely after she tosses me into the nearest medical tent.

The pretty woman chuckles before guiding me over to a nicely prepared cot. "I'm Sarafina. I'm here to fix whatever damage you might've obtained during the joust."

The alarm in my mind sets off. If I take off my armor this woman will know that I am also a woman. Which means my cover will have been blown. She could then call the guards and have me arrested. Then I will be tried by the royal court and killed. My life very well might end abruptly.

Fuck that.

I attempt to get back on my feet but instantly fall back down on account of my sudden dizzy spell.

"Actually, I think I'm quite alright here." I try to sound sure of myself. But this woman is not believing a word I say.

She goes as far as to push me back down with the shoulder. The surprising physical contact makes a flush of heat travel to that area of my side. The pain is so much that I bite the inside of my cheek to keep from crying out.

I will not be weak.

"You are not fine just as I suspected. Let me look and stop this bleeding" Sarafina moves to untie the leather knots holding my armor in place. I yank away from her in a huff.

"No. I'm fine, honestly. I don't need help. Thank you for the offer though." With that, I make my way out of the tent with a triumphant grin. I cannot hide it despite my bleeding form. I won. I'm off to the final trial.

Sarafina crosses her arms. A skeptical look on her graceful face. "If you need any help, I usually assist the physician at the castle."

"Thank you but I won't need any help of yours." I refuse to

give her a second glance before stalking off.

~ ~ ~

I find Artis and his wife sitting inside the Yellow Piggle with worried faces.

"Why so blue?" I ask after slamming the front door behind me. I can even feel how cold my flesh is. Am I dying?

Aunty Kurty yelps in surprise when I fall face-first onto the dirty floor. My body gives out with no warning. My ribs are being consumed in internal flames. I think I've bled all I can. However, I still manage to make the floor turn red and sticky.

"Why didn't you let Sarafina examine you?" I don't care to ask how they know of the woman who tried to help me.

Artis is at my side instantly, being careful not to spill more of me. I find relief in sitting at the nearest table.

"She wanted to look at the damage. I couldn't let her see me as a woman. It would ruin everything I've accomplished since being here." I admit, a shy flush erupting over my neck and face.

Kurty's eyes go wide in realization. "Of course, we didn't think of that possibility."

"Oh, it's alright. I'll be okay. Just want some much needed sleep. Perhaps a few stitches." I chuckle. That silly laugh then turns into a frightening cough. It scares me the way I struggle to regain my composure.

This may not be a simple injury but somehow, I can already feel the magic inside of my chest wield my flesh to weave back together. Healing will take time away from training. Damn!

"I shall whip up some broth. Stay here and don't strain yourself. Artis, you patch her up." Kurty orders me and her husband before marching away into the kitchen.

I smile at her motherly nature. Though I welcome it dearly. The truest form of motherhood has been graced upon me. I plan to take all that I can.

Artis gets on his knees to peer into my tired eyes. His big tough guy act slipping away further each day. I haven't spoken a word about it. Don't plan to either. It is strange to see this man so caring, caring like a father. This saddens me greatly.

My father should be kneeling here to comfort me, offering comforting expressions instead of Artis.

But my father would want me to take all the help. To welcome every piece of advice with an open heart. There is no need to shy away from caring for people.

"I'm proud of you, Anna. We've got one more trial. Fight that man with everything you got." He speaks to me fiercely. Not once does his harsh glare falter.

I'm suddenly glad to have found the Yellow Piggle. These two weeks have felt like two years.

My whole future depends on this upcoming sword duel. There is no going back for me. That was never an option in the first place. I need to complete the last trial. Every ounce of my soul craves to be a knight. I won't go out without a fight. They will have to strike me down with full force to let that happen.

"When do I learn to fight?" I ignore the ticking sting in my side. Refuse to acknowledge the amount of dark red blood I've lost.

I'm not even worried about how terribly my chest aches. A monstrous shake enters my lungs. I simply ignore every piece of me that hurts like a bitch.

Artis scoffs. Which earns him a whimper from me.

"You aren't going back on that training field for a few days."

I stare down at him with shock in my gaze. "What does that even mean? I can't waste any time. This is my final test, Artis!"

I try pleading my case, but he isn't buying it.

Seems like Kurty saves his ass when She struts out with a steaming bowl in her hands.

It was a great distraction for me, at least for now. The smell of carrots and chicken wafts into my nose. A snarl from deep within my stomach fills the tavern, like a mighty roar. They better not think that I will simply forget this little argument.

However, I guess eating my problems away is a better option.

Seventeen

I wait and wait for either Kurty or Artis to bust into my room to demand practice. But neither appears. No one shouts at me from down in the kitchen. But eventually, I am summoned.

It isn't until early Thursday morning that Artis comes knocking on my door rather loudly. The sudden noise causes me to jolt up from the bed. I ignored every pain in my body still left over from the last trial I endured.

I never felt so alive once shoving my bruised feet into my boots again. Being on bed rest was absolute torture. Getting back on my sea legs is amazing.

We march to the training grounds with confidence. Or at least I attempt to. I was in bed for a few days without any sort of exercise.

Causing my form to grow stiff. Stunting the growth of my newly surfacing muscles.

I unwillingly feel out of my element once again. Hopefully, I shall just fall back into the swing of things. Though I don't really think it's possible as I struggle to retrieve the final weapon from its sheath. That little ounce of confidence I have quickly vanishes into nothing.

~ ~ ~

"I can get you a better sword if you'd like?" Artis folds his arms as I begin to wipe my battered weapon down with a white cloth.

I glare at him and scoff. There's no way I'd give this masterpiece up. Not after begging my village's blacksmith for it all those weeks ago.

"Kiss my ass." That's all I say and continue to make sure I see my white hair in the reflection. Shining a knight's weapon is an important part of knighthood as well. Or at least that's what the stories say.

Sir Argson, the grandest knight, would often shine his sword before any battle. That was my father's favorite tale.

Artis grins at my sailor-like ways. "I thought it not kind to curse in front of ladies?"

He uses my own words against me. I drop the cleaning cloth. A deadly look graces my face.

"How dare you?" I practically bark at him while standing.

"I'm just trying to understand," Artis says with a smile. I want to whack it off his face.

But I know he's doing all of this on purpose. He chuckles a throaty gust, eyeing me curiously. As if he were a grandfather watching over his only grandchild.

I can see the longing look. How he and Kurty must have tried for children many times. But the heavens wouldn't grant them a little girl or boy. No matter how hard they prayed to the old gods. Maybe they even tried pleading with the Seekers. Deadly beings who know all that concerns every magic.

I lift the heavy sword into the moist air. The kingdom had been gifted with rain recently. Now all the grounds are nice and wet and ready for action.

The weapon sits heavy in my hands. As if it were not meant to be there within my shaking grasp. However, that does not sway me. I shall not falter again. I almost did not make it in the last trial. Still, I'm surprised I didn't die from the loss of almost all my blood.

But I know at this moment that there's nothing holding me back. I will participate in this duel and gain knighthood. All I have to do now is learn how to wield this sword. To perform such sacred warrior dances with a blade in my hands.

I peer at my mentor hoping to catch a glimpse of any pride in his eyes. I don't think I see any. How disappointing.

"What am I to do now?" I shrug my shoulders.

Artis grunts and retrieves his own sword. A blade much nicer than mine. There are no chipped edges or curves in the weapon. It even has a nice shine to it while mine is still covered in rust.

"Normally, children must start out with a wooden sword. You are no child. So, we must begin with the real thing. Let's hope you are worthy to wield such a weapon." He explains to me whilst twirling his sword.

I notice how swiftly he moves with it. As if this is not the first time a weapon such as that is in his hands. Excitement makes my skin tingle.

"Place your feet right, like this." He tells me. I watch Artis get into a fight-ready position smoothly.

I'm obliged to mimic it the best I can.

Artis makes sure I'm watching closely before moving on. "Carefully, raise the tip to point in that direction."

Then I follow each instruction. Matching each twist of his elbows and wrists.

He encourages me to run through a simple routine quite a few times. To really get the hang of wielding this piece of ironwork. But once it comes to the much harder and quicker stances, I fight with grand might to keep upright. Trying to balance such an uneven sword is difficult. It wasn't made for my bruised hands. But I'm too stubborn to admit it out loud.

After a while, Artis voices that he wants to start fighting. It makes me want to puke. Nerves eat away at my insides. The recovering slice in my side still stings whenever I move too quickly. I sure do hope the stitches don't pop.

What else can possibly happen?

"Pick up your elbow as you swing," Artis orders me after my fifth try at slashing the sword in his direction.

I'm grateful the steel clashes together a few times. A few iron sparks fly around us from the contact. Now it's all down to keeping up with an opponent.

"I'm doing that." I bark through gritted teeth.

I make another attempt to jab the blade into his blind spot. Artis catches it just in time. We collide with one another,

127

making a loud clanking noise echo between us. The vibration causes my skin to crawl savagely.

Artis smiles again. "Your defense is getting better. Remember to knock your opponent's sword to the ground. That is when you'll know you have won."

I force myself to remember those words. No matter what I need to get his sword out of his hands. It's the only way I can survive the trial. Though I think it is rather cowardly. At this point, being a coward and going for the sword instead of a man is the only option.

Might as well make it count.

~ ~ ~

After a few hours, I start to grow tired. My body is beginning to slow down rapidly. I'm so drowsy that my sword slips from my fingers and sinks into the soft ground.

Artis sighs while taking in my exhausted form. I don't want to appear weak in front of him. However, I can't help the tired spell from taking over me.

Drained by all I had to offer this week.

A small ache enters my chest. I need to lay down and fast before I meet a mouth full of wet dirt.

Artis tells me how I'm expected to be in a better mood for the next night. I don't feel like arguing with him about his overly joyous tone.

Nothing can be done to ease his boyish excitement. I'm not sure I even want to ruin it.

All I care about is getting back to my precious cot. The thought of soft cozy sheets makes my skin tingle in the best way. The idea of crashing into soft pillows causes a smile to rise upon my crusted lips.

Suddenly, the walk back to the Yellow Piggle has become faster than usual. I must jog just to keep up with the tavern owner.

Kurty waits at the front door tonight. A pleasant grin plastered on her face. I know instantly that something is very wrong. She never waits up for us anymore.

"Crowlen and his men stopped by." She confesses to both her husband and me.

I stop dead in my tracks. My wide eyes look all around, searching for any possible sign of that crazed beautiful man lurking about.

Is he still somehow watching us? His sour taste still lingers in the air around us. It settles uncomfortably on my tongue.

"Oh, yeah? What was he looking for now?" Artis kisses his wife upon the cheek. I turn to look anywhere but at them with a blush atop my face.

The older woman giggles. "The last thing he had been searching for."

Somehow that gives me a sliver of relief. Good to know he isn't looking for anything that might upset my plans. I can't have that.

"Get inside the both of you." The mother hen orders us with a stern voice. Neither of us utters a word against her. I smile brightly.

I never thought my adult life would be filled with great people. I have even made friends with the locals.

A few booth owners in Celeste Square adore me. I've started to play around with the village children in my free time. We act out glorious adventures that consist of dragons and witches.

Maybe living within the walls of Thrallen is what my father

wanted after all.

Eighteen

"Put your shoulder into it!" Artis growls at me as I shove my sword into a barrel of hay.

My wobbly movements cause me to miss the red-painted circle by mere inches. A hiss flies from my mouth. Tears of frustration leak down the sides of my face. I can taste the salt from the sweat that slips down onto my dry tongue.

"I'm trying." I snarl after a fifth attempt. I still miss it repeatedly. His continuous verbal jabs are not helping to provide me with any useful motivation.

Artis tries demonstrating again. I'm not paying a bit of

attention to him. My focus is too strong on my own weapon. With each faulty strike the more I grow angry at myself and these silly dreams.

"I cannot do this." I yelp after my sword slips down out of my hands, leaving my fingertips numb.

It crashes right into the ground. I'll have to clean the mud off later. Right now, I need a damn break. So, I sit down with terrible grace. Not caring that my breeches are getting soaked from the damp soil beneath me. There are too many other annoying things to worry about.

The owner of the Yellow Piggle roughly rubs his face. An irritated expression he shoots at me. There is no care in me about it. Water has been the only source of energy in my mind. A slice of beef pie also sounds delicious. The thought makes my stomach rumble. All this fighting is starving me.

So, I fetch the nearest canteen and drain it completely dry. Not daring to clean my drenched chin of stray drops. I'm a brute at this moment. Artis can't even begin to imagine what must be going through my head. He isn't going to ask about it either.

"You certainly aren't going to win with that fucking attitude." He says to me firmly. Watching me slosh around fueled his temper.

I aim a glare at him, hoping it will somehow cause his big head to catch fire. "Oh yeah? What attitude am I supposed to have?"

Artis curses. Clearly, he's taken aback by my foul presence. I look and act awful towards him. I guess me being ladylike is a damn long stretch as far as Artis is concerned.

And yet nothing in me lets me give a damn.

"Definitely not that one. At least try and act ecstatic.

You've completed the first two Knight Trials. This is a major accomplishment for any nobleman. Especially for a woman such as you." Artis starts his fancy speech. I've heard it a thousand times before. It's getting a bit old.

I give into a roll of my eyes. His words are pointless. He watches my gaze turn cold. It's truly one of self-pity. He knows he must get rid of it quickly before it's too late.

The much older man takes a seat in front of me, crossing his legs in a child-like way. I find him to be mocking me almost. Artis is a bear who uses forceful words and intense gazes to induce motivation. I'm beginning to wonder if he will ever give up on me like I desperately want to.

Artis suddenly takes both my busted hands in his. Newly formed blisters and bloodied cuts cover my darkened knuckles. I hiss through gritted teeth as his rough fingertips skim the sensitive skin. The harsh sting adds to my internal fire. And my side isn't completely healed yet either. This morning I had to gently wipe away crusted blood from the cut. It was rather painful.

"Listen to what I'm saying." Artis begins again. I make sure I peer into his oldish eyes. Maybe I do need to hear this. There's nothing else I can do but listen carefully and admit defeat. It seems to be the time for it. I won't dare try to avoid it any longer.

"You've walked to Thrallen from another kingdom that couldn't give a damn about its people. Raced into woods so unfamiliar due to a phantom scream. Met the king and his inner circle by accident. Even battled against an enchanted plant with absolutely no experience with a sword." His words strike me deep within my aching heart.

Those tears I had from anger now turn into ones of sour

emotional pain. It's hard to focus on him through the salty rain I produce.

"And don't even get me started about meeting your worst enemy. Crowlen will slit your throat himself. Yet you've escaped him more than you know." Artis sounds so sure.

It seems that someone wanted me to cross paths with Artis. Why else would I be willing to accept this kind of pep talk over and over again? There is some force out there who planned this. I can't tell whether I should thank it or not.

I can easily sense him thinking of this as well. It's no secret how grateful I am for him and his wife's support. Whatever he's hiding from me must have happened a long time ago. Aunty Kurty tends to make it seem like I have been some type of redemption for them.

There will be no doubt of me doing my best to prove myself to them.

"You're right. I'm upset over the wrong reasons. I've come too far to give up now. No more complaining will come from me. That is a promise." I get up on my feet, making sure I appear confident. Even when I am deathly afraid on the inside.

Artis smiles, but it's lopsided. His thick mustache flicks up with his lips. A sparkle washes over his eyes once more.

I know this sword duel will be a matter of life and death. Whoever I'm meant to face won't stop until I'm no longer breathing. This is going to be the fight of my life. So, why not take the bull by the horns?

~ ~ ~

For many hours into the late night and early morning, me and Artis work harder than ever before. I do everything I am told and push my limits to the max. There is no complaint from me, just as I promised.

I will my bent blade to move as if it's the real thing.

Eventually, it truly feels like me and my sword are one of the same.

Nineteen

This might be the worst morning I've had throughout my stay in Thrallen.

I wake to extreme pains in my lower belly. A flush of very warm goo shoots down the insides of my thighs. My aches only grow worse when I take in the sight of fresh red blood trailing down my legs.

"Shit!" My sudden curse word is going to be the least of my worries. I wasn't expecting my monthly bleed until next week.

There's nothing I can do to delay this. So, the only thing I can do is press a thick absorbent cloth down on the inside of my undergarment and pray to the Seekers that there won't be any red accidents.

I hope that no one will notice that there's something off about me. My best bet is to ignore the cramps long enough to go through the trial. If I make it out alive I'll ask Kurty if she has anything to ease them away.

Aunty Kurty hints to me that she knows something odd is going on with a wink. I eat my breakfast of oats and berries in silence. A flush of embarrassment is heavy on my cheeks and sides of my neck. My empty bowl should have been a good enough thanks.

~ ~ ~

This day is different from the others. Besides the bloody accident from this morning.

Usually, everyone is buzzing with excitement. But not this time, not this day. No one seems happy to be at the final trial. This worries me greatly. The pit of my stomach is only growing deeper.

How am I to be ecstatic when no one else is?

Of course, there is no need to be giddy. None of Kurty's words of encouragement make me better. I'm too worried about having to whack a sword from someone else's hands. The thought causes nasty moths to fly around in my guts.

Doubt with a snarl lingers in my mind. I shove it down as deep as I can. Whatever it takes to not strike myself out when I haven't even gotten to the arena.

Artis came by earlier to let them know I will be competing last. My opponent isn't known yet. The judges still need to fill the empty spot from what he gathered.

Which gives me some time to prepare. To allow me to receive a small pep talk. I'll take anything to bring my nerves down to rest in a lake of calm.

"You are Anna Scarrow. The daughter of a brave and honest man. You can win this trial. You must." I can't believe this is all I manage to come up with while waiting outside the arena as people file into the stands.

Really, how much more pathetic can I be?

A few small children whose parents guide them inside stop briefly to wave at me and the other trial competitors. I fight the urge to return the gesture, keeping my tight closed fists at my sides. There can't be any room in my mind to let in silly distractions. No matter how much I want to meet their sweet and innocent enthusiasm.

It's very important that I maintain my manly appearance.

Then a splendid idea jolts into my head when I least expect it.

I excuse myself when no one is looking in my direction to hurry back to the Yellow Piggle. Artis gives me a funny look, his thick brow raised high in question. I shake my head, silently telling him not to panic. He shoots me a wink as I hurry away.

My calves burn from this ridiculous speed of walking. A few folks glance at me, observing my strange behavior. I refuse to meet their eyes as I make it to the tavern with a little over an hour to spare.

I'm out of breath by the time I get to my room. Hunting for my small mirror does not take long. It's scraping my fake beard off that takes the most time. Having to wipe off all the hard work Kurty put into her art is almost sad. But I do not give myself the chance to mourn this.

138

I choose not to fight as my false persona, Mason Triscan. But this time I shall be all Anna Scarrow underneath this armor. I meant to do this since the start. As I told my father I would. I would be knighted as a woman whether they all know it or not. Having to fake being a man forever isn't the goal.

One day I will be able to reveal such truths.

One day. Just not now.

Taking out the leather strand holding my hair back is thrilling. Being able to feel the locks swing above my shoulders is surely everything. The length is still short enough to where it rests right underneath the helmet. But I do redraw a small mustache. At least I'm trying to be careful.

I'll have to remove that head protector later after my victory. No need for anyone to question my gender now. It's not the right time to reveal such things.

The truth will be too much for many. Most would never understand why I have been doing this. Not yet at least.

I sprint all the way back to the arena grounds. Armor clashing together with each quick step I take. My breathing labored. Kurty and her husband wait impatiently for my much-anticipated arrival.

I spot them looking all around for any sight of me. A smile sprouts on my face.

"Thank the Seekers you're here. The horn will blow soon. Be careful, Anna. Don't lose hope. Not ever again." Kurty straightens my shiny breastplate one last time. There's no time to say any more than that. But it's more than enough for me.

"I shall see you after my victory." I grin even though they can't see. My helmet blocks their view of my severely flushed face.

"Kick his ass," Artis smirks like a madman. I nod in return. Feeling the same amount of glee.

As if destiny knocks on my the front of my heart, the horn blasts away.

I march to my new life. The life of a knight waits for me just inside the arena. The thought makes my mouth water oh so deliciously.

~ ~ ~

Cheers fill my thumping ears. Waves of people jump in the wooden stands. The vibrations encourage the seats to raddle like bells. Streamers of yellow and brown flow in the stale winds. Children scream away in delight. I enjoy these sights and sounds.

However, every ounce of happiness I hold suddenly pours out of me.

King Kasper rises from his throne to calm the crowd. Crowlen is nowhere in sight. Panic sets in my bones. Why would he miss the last trial? This isn't right at all. He must be doing something sinister to skip an event such as the final Knight Trial.

I've got a bad feeling about this.

"My people, may I present to you Mason Triscan. Our second to last opponent on the right." His beautiful blue eyes peer down at me. He gracefully aims his arms in my direction.

As a way of creating a strong presence. The people go wild at the mention of my false name. I can't find the motivation in me to smile back at them. Something about this trial feels wrong. I hope I'm just nervous and can get over this sudden paranoia.

Kasper speaks again. This time with a gracious amount of pride fleeing from his words. "Unfortunately, the judges and I miscalculated the number of men that would actually make it through the trials. We have less than was expected originally. Meaning that Mason Triscan wouldn't have anyone to duel against. But my most trusted advisor and royal warlock has volunteered to go against him instead. What a true team player he has always been."

Excuse me? What the fuck did he just say?

I stagger in the corner in utter shock. I had wondered what that dangerous man had been up to of late. Now actually knowing that he means to fight me makes everything a hundred times worse.

Oh, Seekers. He knows. *He knows what I am.*

This is his ultimate plan. He found me out. How could I have let this happen? If he does not kill me in this trial, then he will either burn me to a crisp in Celeste Square or drown me in an icy river. And I doubt he will wait for any permission from the king.

This new problem seriously puts my monthly bleeding to shame. Not even the warm gathering down there and hardy muscle spasms can be considered an issue now. Hot tears spring to my eyes. Sniffing harshly, I refuse to let them fall.

Thrallen's people cry out again in glee. Their cheers go nonstop. One of their greatest protectors is going to put on a good show for them.

They must all know that.

I'm going to die today, I've concluded. Nothing can sway that possibility. It's inevitable.

I'm certain that Crowlen did this on purpose. Must have messed with silly paperwork. He's been horrible to me since day one. Of course, I figured he suspected something. And I was right after all.

Why else would he do this? I had been doomed from the start.

I watch as the opposite end of the arena goes berserk. The opposing doors sway open to reveal a set of masterful armor.

I've never felt so puny and insignificant in my life as I do now.

Crowlen is covered in raven-black plates. Each piece is carefully branded with silver markings and red crystals. His helmet matches in every way, raven wings kissing the sides of it. The only difference is that the eye guards are a deep iridescent purple. His beauty is brought on by the Seekers themselves.

As if they pulled him from their sacred lake. I'm not sure if I should believe it or not.

However, those deadly red eyes glow against the darkness. I start to feel my world crumble to my feet. Every little piece is being pulled into the ground. Slowly. Painfully.

"At the sound of the horn battle will commence. Do well, Mason Triscan. No need to praise you, warlock," King Kasper beams down upon me. His chuckle does not help to ease those chilled feelings that spark within me.

I want to run away screaming in terror. Maybe a metaphorical tail between my legs would be wise.

The nasty warlock approaches the center ground. I follow in his steps with my shoulders pulled back, meeting him halfway.

The evil stare he shoots me gives a pretty good hint of what he thinks of all this. He knows exactly who's underneath this new armor and shield.

Not even a second later a frightening sound echoes from

the horn. It plants a string of self-doubt and fear up my spine. Everything is lost before it begins.

All my hard work simply goes down the drain.

Crowlen instantly lifts his sword for a swing, his left foot jutting out in front of him. Surprisingly, I avoid his strike with my shield. The metal collides and creates a ricochet effect. I feel it in my elbow. I inwardly cringe from the nauseating experience.

He keeps coming with his blade repeatedly. That damned sword attempts to clash with my head, making me duck like crazy. I have no choice but to scamper away like a coward.

This is probably a good chance to find his weak spot before he slices me in two.

Though it seems he knows just where to hit me. Crowlen doesn't falter once. I need to figure something out before it's too late. Perhaps I should in fact use my training and fucking use my sword! That's what it's for.

His body moves swiftly. Crowlen is a pretty black swan dancing atop a broken lake. If there was time I'd sit back and watch him do this dance. He's quite handsome.

It's as if a miracle answers me. The battle-driven man misses a step from his rash actions, causing him to barely miss my left arm. This is the opening I've been waiting for!

I use this wonderful opportunity to raise my own sword high in the air. I barely have a moment to bring it down with all my womanly might. The tip of the blade lands right on his side.

"Fuck!" Crowlen curses as the sword pierces his vulnerable armpit. A weak spot.

I pull back my weapon and watch Crowlen's dark red blood flicker in the air. A few drops landed on my silver boot and breastplate. The scent of fresh iron fills my nostrils. I inhale the smell as fuel for my confidence. It tastes better than his magic.

However, because of the look of his deadly eyes and the sudden silence of the crowd, this might have been a huge mistake on my part. I involuntarily gulp.

The people go still. A few gasps circle around us. No one expected me to make a silly blow. But they were wrong to judge. And so was I.

Crowlen slowly stops his attack. He tilts his head. I watch a fire soar within his eyes, their red color now glowing bright like a blazing star. He wants to really kill me. I won't let him.

I back up slightly, planting my feet, and getting in the stance of a true fighter. The same one Artis forced me to memorize. My limbs move with ease. My muscles remember everything that I've been taught. I want to thank Crowlen now with a massive hug.

"You don't belong here." He seethes just loud enough for only me to hear.

I smile wickedly. I could have sworn he had seen it too. "The only way I leave this place is if I burn on the stake." This time I don't use my forced manly voice. I want him to hear the real me. So that he knows what someone else's victory sounds like.

In the heat of the moment, both of us rush toward each other. Swords and shields in trembling hands. Terrifying expressions grace our faces.

I don't hold back my next attack. With this strike, I push my shoulder into it with all my energy.

I waste no time in watching my blade slice across his knee, somehow it cuts through his armor. Crowlen yelps out in pain. His discomfort is the last thing on my mind.

144

Maybe I crave it just a tad bit. How sinister that's to think about.

He manages to nip my side pretty well. I stumble forward while doing my best to ignore the puncture wound from the jousting match that's been reopened and now bleeding. It's not a burning sensation like before. It feels like my skin is involuntarily pulled apart by tongs.

Thank Seekers I don't faint and fall on my face from more blood loss.

It would have been embarrassing if Crowlen chopped off my head. A pretty sight that wouldn't be.

Our intense battle continues for another hour at most. Both Crowlen and I grow tired. There are no signs of either one of us giving up. I refuse to stall and rest for a moment. He knows this and it makes him more angry. Good.

That's when I notice the way I can easily beat him. Why haven't I thought of this before?

"Had enough yet?" He asks after slamming his weapon down next to my foot. Crowlen managed to miss my toes.

I twirl away. My side has stopped leaking blood. "Never. I'm surprised an old man such as yourself hasn't doubled over from a heart attack."

My chuckle seems to truly irritate him.

I know that my plan will work.

His eyes darken as he studies me.

"Let us finish this." His raspy voice goes hoarse. Crowlen's on the verge of pure terror. I grin.

"As you wish." I get close enough to whisper into his helmet. My silky breath fans against the raven wing. Goosebumps flash over his skin. Too bad I can't tell if he's squirming or not.

He thinks he can snatch my shield from our proximity. I

instantly see him go for it. His attention is no longer on his sword.

I then elbow his wrist. Crowlen isn't expecting sudden physical contact from me. Making him lose hold of the hilt. His dark-bladed sword crusted with my blood slips down, sticking upright in the dirt.

A horrid roar escapes from his lips. Crowlen shoves me back hard enough that I go crashing to the ground.

His magic quickly pours out of him. I gag from the nasty flavor. Sour apples flushing my taste buds. The exact opposite of mine. It's dark and unmeasurable. Crowlen wants to kill me, and he doesn't give a shit about how it's done.

The warlock hovers over me. "You have lost."

My eyes open wider as he lifts his palm. Dark red flames the shade of blood start to swarm around me. They lick at my heels like hungry wolves.

I want to scream bloody murder. But no sound comes from my lips. I can't hear myself think.

"Halt!" King Kasper's anxious voice rings out from his booth.

The mystical fire abruptly stops consuming me. It feels like I've been boiled alive. Sweat drips down beneath my helm and a few burns coat my legs. Crowlen slowly backs away. His harsh breathing echoes out into the stilled arena. Though his magic does not fade completely. It wraps around his shoulders like a deadly embrace. This warlock is a monster.

He only snarls, stomping away in extreme defeat. Crowlen flees out the arena door at the other end of us. His velvet cape breezes behind him in his tracks.

I can't even imagine what he'll do to me if he catches me alone after this.

I rest on the ground with a racing heart. It takes me a

moment to realize that I've won my last trial. But at what cost? My insides are numb to any victorious feeling.

Kasper speaks again but this time with pure wonder. "Welcome to the Knights of Thrallen, Mason Triscan!"

The people of Thrallen rise to their feet and pump their joyous fists in the air. And all I can think about is how guilty I am about winning when I should be dead.

Twenty

Crowlen

I throw my scratched helmet across my bedchamber, causing a crash of glass and books. My workspace is now completely destroyed, again. A shattered bottle of blue ink drips away onto the black-tiled floor.

Fantastic. Another stain for Coven to clean.

A howl of brewing anger escapes me. My body shakes from the rage that fills my wicked heart. How could I have been so stupid? I'm a damn fool!

I should have known what that pesky girl was up to. But once I finally figured out Anna was the witch, I knew to act quickly. Today was supposed to be the day I should have ended her fucking life.

Though I didn't think it possible for her to actually beat me in a duel. Utter humiliation flutters inside my chest. The people of Thrallen watched me be struck down like a blade of grass. Oh, how horrible indeed.

This day is not supposed to have ended up like this.

None of them know she's a woman. And that fact pisses me off greatly. It's so obvious that I suspected this almost instantly. Even I can see her strange and rare features. Anna Scarrow is definitely a descendant of an ancient line of magic wielders. Yet I can't seem to figure out which one yet.

Another problem for another time.

I continue to throw small pieces of furniture with the little energy I have left. I only stop when Coven, the royal messenger, and my terrible personal assistant, rushes inside the room. I let out a snarl.

Not a good time for this annoying rat to disturb me. Doesn't he know I can easily break his neck with a quick snap of my fingers? Brew a potion that will cause his feet to rot and fall off like dead flies?

Coven, the small royal announcer who I wish were dead, gasps, "I cannot believe you battled a real-life witch. What was it like? Did she use her powers on you, Crowlen?"

All these questions make me hot in the face and my skull ache.

"I suggest you stop talking or you shall lose a tongue. I won't be growing it back for you this time."

That shuts up the shorter man rather quickly.

I haven't the time to ponder over that snowy bitch who publicly stumped me. That memory is going to forever scar me. I hate her.

I stomp around once more, calling out strange words in the language of the old magic. A small chant filled with mystical energy to call upon the power inside of me. It works. I can tell all my various cuts from Anna's sword heal in little time and minimal effort.

After a while, I pause abruptly in the middle of the floor. I quickly turn to my little annoying helper. Something within me has awoken and I don't plan to ignore it.

A serious sinister glint appears in my heated eyes. A deadly idea enters my mind. I do not care if it's true or not. I will do anything it takes to take that witch down.

"Anna is here to cause great harm to the king. Alert no one of my findings. I will take care of this problem with my bare hands. Even if that means breaking Thrallen law to get rid of her."

Twenty-One

I'm escorted out of the arena by castle medical assistants. Their looks of worry almost make me sad and somewhat guilty. It wasn't like I got sliced and bruised on purpose. I don't see the helper who almost begged me to stay within the medical tent after the jousting trial.

Me and the other champions are grouped together to avoid the crowds of people who exited the stands in pretty much a riot.

I gain a thumping ache at the front of my skull, messing with my already blurry vision. It's hard to stand upright. All the armor I wear weighs me down horribly. And yet my heart is full of happiness.

Even through our exhaustion, we march in a lenient formation. The day is dying out. Soft rays of the burning orange sun descend upon us. Our different armor shines bright like molten stars on a clear night. And very soon we will all match in bronze armor.

I'm the last of us to enter the castle and yet the first new knight to feel right at home. There's something about these ugly gray brick walls that expresses a familiar sense. I want to inhale all the dust floating around in the air caused by our dirty boots.

Somehow between my gawking a castle guard is assigning us our temporary rooms until the king asks us to volunteer to sleep in the knight barracks. That thought triggers a smile to bloom on my beaten face. However, I'll have to skip that due to me being a woman. Sure, I'll do whatever it takes to participate with my fellow knights, but sleeping in a large room with them just outside the city wall is a bit too risky. Men are more unpredictable than bears.

Though I am the last one to arrive for my room assignment. I'm ultimately gifted the final room. I wonder what it will look like. Perhaps it will be a small broom closet or a massive space. Either way, I'm thrilled.

Once I make it up to the second level and all the way down the hall, I'm genuinely curious. I should be grateful I'm the only floor occupant.

When I open the heavy brown door to my room my jaw drops to the floor. It's more than I could have pictured. A surprisingly beautiful place with a grand window on the far wall. Two massive wardrobes line the wall next to it. Speaking of the walls, I'm surrounded by pale cream-colored bricks. Each one is carefully placed atop the others.

I try very hard to ignore the softness of the queen-size mattress of the four-poster bed. It looks too good to not plop upon. A great canopy of bright yellow silk tops it as well. But what really catches my eye are the new uniforms that have been neatly sprawled across the dark blue blanket.

There are many pieces such as chainmail paired with a pulling string to fit me perfectly and a few sunflower yellow tunics. It's the brown cape sporting a bear crest that makes all my nightmares simply float away. The nicely sewn fabric feels like fluffy clouds beneath my fingertips.

My dreams have finally come true and I'm not sure how to feel about it. Oh, Seekers. I finished the Knight Trials. The realization that my father isn't here to see it hits me hard in the chest.

I cry in silence. Muffled sobs jerk my body as I kneel in the middle of the room. My spirit is consumed with anger and gratitude.

This is everything I ever wanted. I'm inside this amazing castle just rooms away from the other knights and the king. But why do I feel so glum? There must be something wrong with me.

My knighting ceremony is going to take place when the sun disappears. That gives me about an hour to gather my senses. To make myself presentable once again.

I take time to clean myself properly. Carefully wiping my face free of dirt and dried blood. I know just by the bright red color that I will always be different. Magical wielders have unnaturally glowing blood. It's another sign of magic. How no one noticed it during the trials is a wonder to me.

153

But magic isn't what brought me here. It's not magic that helped me win the trials. Magic sure doesn't make me, well, me.

I sniffle and turn to lovely knight garments on the bed.

It feels oddly familiar to wear such a cape. I believe I was always meant for this. Like I want to fly into the heavens and show my father that it truly happened. He would be proud of me; I know it deep in my heart. That makes me think of Aunty Kurty and Artis.

They will be there for the ceremony. They had promised me. I smile at that. I have some sort of family to cheer me on. And that is everything and more.

~ ~ ~

I stare into the vanity mirror. Drawing on each facial hair with black beard filler I found within the first drawer. It looks like men really enjoy appearing their best. A small quill had been next to it. I use both to look presentable.

I then hear a few officials come down my hallway to fetch other knights. Once after checking a few rooms, they'll realize it's only me here. I better hurry. The knights aren't going to witness each other's special night. I don't know if that's a good thing or not. But I wait patiently for my turn once I finish getting ready.

Not too long later a fist lands on the door. "Mason Triscan, the king himself has summoned you. Come now." A new voice calls out to me.

Butterflies fill my gut. This is it.

I walk alongside a small boy down the hall. He wears Thrallen colors with a smile on his face. He must be in training to be a messenger. A dangerous profession in this world. I don't say one word about my concerns. What I've done may get me killed one day.

I traveled down many perfectly carved stone steps leading to checkered flooring. There isn't time to stop and admire each portrait of the royals. I'll have to investigate them some other time.

Soon I arrive in front of glorious brown doors with a bear and more sunflowers carved into the wood. They're tall. So tall that they start from the ceilings. There are two guards posted before either door. They pull them open to reveal a hall filled with people.

My heart stops beating for a moment.

King Kasper rises from his throne formed from gold solid stone. A few places are trimmed in pure yellow. My breath is taken away by the number of people that occupy the small wood stands on both sides of the room. So many smiling faces. Children admiring every step forward I take.

I spot Artis and his wife midway down the fancy red carpet. My nerves grow fierce as I approach the steps leading to a platform.

No other royal Madlock is in sight. Kasper is the last of his line. I assume it to be tough standing in front of his people with no one by his side. I too can understand what it feels like to be alone.

The king lifts his arms. Everyone goes silent. As if my body is willing to do so I bend down on one knee. A small red pillow is placed on the bottom step just for this occasion.

I memorized this special ceremony by heart, well mostly. My father told me everything through his stories. So, I took it all in for this moment. All that I could at the age of six.

I watch an elderly man dressed in withered yellow and blue robes hand the Madlock king a rusted sword. Its shine reflects candlelight the best it can.

Kasper holds the sword in his big hands. The muscle in his jaw is ticking away. Once again Crowlen is nowhere in sight. I'm not surprised. I don't give a shit. He isn't important right now.

"Mason Triscan, do you swear to uphold the laws of these lands?" His voice is full of brand-new power. It causes my skin to crawl.

I grin, "I swear."

He too sparks a smile.

"Do you swear to protect my people?" Kasper doesn't attempt to hide his gleaming pearl teeth any longer.

"I swear." I feel my magic rush inside my chest. A great thumping of my heart. Seekers, my whole life spent on knights is finally being rewarded.

Kasper really let his smirk go wild. "Mason Triscan, do you swear to fight for Thrallen?"

It's as if the whole world comes to a stop. I beam brightly.

"I swear it." And just like that, I've won every internal battle I've had with myself. Whatever doubts I once had are now being melted away.

Everyone around me roars. Cheers fill the halls in thunderous waves.

The king performed the bit with the sword. Placing it on each of my shoulders and uttering an ancient chant only the kings of Seekers Land are allowed to know.

He then says, "Sir Mason, Knight of Thrallen."

~ ~ ~

A splendid party breaks out amongst the people and new knights. Food and music are requested at once by the king. So that's what flows within this grand space.

Aunty Kurty and Artis sought me out quickly. They find me leaning against a stone pillar, gazing at the crowded dance floor.

"Can't believe it can you?" Artis asks when he notices my blank expression.

It soon becomes one of excitement. "I can believe it just fine. I'm thinking of my first patrol or Stars tournament."

Of course, my mind would turn to a yearly fun match against fellow knights. A unique tradition only Thrallen holds. I can't wait for my first one.

Kurty scoffs. "Already thinking like a knight. You've been a man too long now. Turn back into the Anna we know." She leans into a whisper that last part.

I chuckle before I turn serious. I watch Crowlen slowly wiggle his way through the crowd straight towards me. When did he get here?

It's hard not to miss his devil eyes.

"Excuse me." I gently move between my mentors to come face to face with the royal warlock. We can only stand and watch this scene unfold. Kurty grips her husband's arm tightly. Her fear for what Crowlen might do to me quickly forms in her head. I can tell by the way her brows scrunch.

Crowlen grins wickedly. "May I have a word?" His voice is calm. Nothing like the tone he had on the fighting ground today. It's much more crystal clear with no menacing aspect.

"Sure." Reluctantly, I follow after Crowlen. We weave through the hordes of celebrating people. I shake a few hands that are thrown at me and smile at the women who give me dazzling eyes.

Yes, I need to be me in this uniform as soon as possible.

He leads me right into the open corridor in front of the throne room doors. No one's around to witness him murder me in cold blood. Not even servers or maids. Truly everyone is too busy partying.

His fake proud expression morphs into one of pure anger. Crowlen grips my shoulders tightly. He pushes me into the nearest wall harshly. I don't have a chance to shove him off. His quick hands are already pulling the leather tie keeping my hair up, allowing the strands to fall in a short wave of snow.

"Should have known a bitch like you would attempt this." Crowlen then uses his black tunic sleeve to angrily rub my chin and upper lip, getting rid of the paint.

I whimper from his force-filled touches. "Get the fuck off of me!" I want to scream louder.

But I know making a scene will ruin my early knighthood before it even really begins.

"Why shouldn't I kill you where you struggle now?" His question is rhetorical.

That doesn't stop me from actually answering it. "Because I've done nothing wrong. There are no rules against women becoming knights." I instantly regret my words. Crowlen doesn't give a damn about me being a knight. That isn't what he's after.

His dark chuckle makes my knees weak. Good thing he still holds me by the shoulders or else I'd collapse in a blubbering heap.

"No, that isn't really the issue here. You should've been smarter. No woman with magic is allowed here in Thrallen. So why did you come here? Answer me!"

This isn't the time to have this argument.

A very frantic messenger boy runs down the hall straight into Crowlen's side. He stumbles onto his backside, sweat drips down his young face. He must have run all the way from the post tower. The warlock drops his hold on me to hoist the boy up. I step out of the way. My interest overwhelms my fear of the warlock.

"What the hell do you want?" He asks the frightened boy.

Without thinking I whack the back of his shoulder. He sneers at my touch. Of course, I ignore it. He doesn't have to be rude to him.

"I've retrieved word from the scouts in Pucnasia. The queen is on the march to Thrallen. We are all doomed."

Well, now that is a good reason to completely forget the possibility of being killed by Crowlen.

Twenty-Two

C rowlen holds the boy's wrist in a tight grip. All three of us storm into the hall of drunken people. King Kasper sits on his throne watching everyone dance to mystical tunes.

His happy face glooms quickly. He rises on quick feet and calls for those around to quiet down. His subjects do just as he asks.

I don't know what to think as Crowlen sprints up the steps to whisper into the king's ear. Every twist of Kasper's face makes this situation worse.

So many thoughts run in my head.

"My people, I must order you all to your homes for the remainder of this night. I shall speak with you all in Celeste Square tomorrow at midday. No need for panic. Knights of Thrallen please stay within these walls. We have a lot to discuss."

Soon the throne room goes silent. The many cheery people flee back into the streets. Most likely to find any open taverns to continue the celebration. That might be the best thing for them.

Me and my fellow knights line up together in a grand formation. We create a unified front even if most of us have no idea in which way to properly stand. All of us are on edge. I bet every single one of our hearts is beating fast, wanting to burst our chest due to anticipation.

The king paces back and forth before his throne. Possibly contemplating on how to share the news. I may already know what's been said but I have no idea how he plans to address it. And that's what scares me.

"I've spoken of a possible war with Queen Pearlina of Pucnasia for a while. However, it appears that she's made the first move. An army of thousands is on its way. She leads them herself." His once bright features turn grim. His eyes darken.

A few gasps are made. They all knew this day would come. I haven't even considered this. I've been too busy trying to get into my knighthood. But now is the time for all of us to prove ourselves. Show exactly why we made it through the trials and joined the ranks of King Kasper's army, whatever is left of it.

The true noblemen here have trained with their fathers since birth. Me and my father didn't have much time or skill for anything like that. Artis is the best thing I've got.

The king doesn't look pleased with this sudden realization. I don't honestly blame him.

"She caught a very important spy of mine. Sir Bullskin has been compromised, beaten, and starved for weeks from what I've gathered. That bitch of a queen sent him back to us with a message. He managed to tell us her plan before taking his last breath of Thrallen air. She and her army will be waiting at the mountains bordering Thrallen. We've got less than four days to meet them. There is no time to properly prepare you." King Kasper's voice booms in the throne room.

I can't do anything but listen to his chilling words. All of this is suddenly too real. Never did I think I would be in an actual war. Not yet at least. Being a knight already means business. Just as I wished for.

"Go. Pack your travel bags. We meet outside the gates an hour after midday."

~ ~ ~

I'm stopped by Crowlen on the way out of the throne room.

"You shall be in my troop. Your magic will come in handy." He tells me as we stalk to the staircase leading up to the second level of the castle.

There are no objections to be made.

"I'm not sure that's a good idea. My magic is unpredictable and most of the time doesn't like it when I try to force it out of me." Well, that's almost true.

I haven't learned to properly use it. If I try to summon it out on the battlefield, I could hurt someone. And I will not

162

cause the deaths of innocents. I won't be a witch that I know Crowlen sees me as.

"Pearlina's magic doesn't match mine in the slightest, but her cunning nature makes up for what it lacks. If push comes to shove, then I'll need whatever fucking power you possess to be on my side. I only hope that what I felt that day in Celeste Square is as deadly as I think it is. Don't die in that valley before you become valuable to me." Then the warlock rushes out of my sight, even bothering to knock into my shoulder roughly. I almost fall against the wall but manage to prevent that using my hands to hold me steady.

I run back to my bedchamber at the far end of the hall. My heart races wildly. Tears of horror flow down my face. I don't care about the leftover beard paint that drips down my chin.

Shouts echo from behind me. Guards inform knights of when they must exit the castle and where their troops will be located.

One knocks upon my door to tell me the same. I yell back that I understand the orders. Though I sound like a man who's been smoking a pipe for most of his life.

It's somewhat difficult to determine what I can use with all that I came to the castle with. Which of course were all the clothes on my body.

After a few minutes of searching the room, I find a hidden compartment within the first wardrobe.

I'm greeted with a glorious blinding sight. There are many kinds of different knives, hatchets, bows, and arrows that fill the drawer.

This room is fully stocked with weapons. So much more than I can even think about carrying.

I jump on my toes in excitement with fists pumping in the

air. A wondrous feeling now seeping into my bones. Knowing that I have other small tools besides my sword is more than enough.

I spend a while selecting which knives can fit in my new boots best. Then having to figure out how I will hide a machete behind my breastplate is a slight struggle. But I come up with an idea anyway.

Soon I have the perfect setup for battle. I hope I will remember having these secret tools at my side in the middle of this impending fight.

I have just placed my folded uniform atop the travel pack when a knock sounds on the door.

The rushing of the blood in my veins pauses for a moment.

I'm dressed in a nightgown and suddenly feel too exposed. I found it in one of the drawers of the wardrobe. It might have been meant for a large man, but I discovered some use for it. If I'm to be living here, then I'll need to fetch my belongings from the Yellow Piggle.

I make no sudden movements. Maybe whoever is at the door might think I'm asleep and walk back down the hall. No sounds of footsteps lead away from the door. I'm not in the clear.

"Mason?" The voice of Crowlen sets my body on fire. Anger fills my chest in an instant.

He doesn't give me a chance to answer. Crowlen yanks the door open to storm inside, breaking the lock in the process.

My eyes scan over his perfectly dark tunic and matching pants. The top buttons are undone to reveal white flesh covered in slight chest hair. Even his long hair lays over his shoulders in raven waves. I hate how wonderful he looks at any time of the day. It's not natural.

164

"Can't seem to stay away from me, can you? Please, don't make a habit of visiting me during the night." I say whilst crossing my arms over my chest. Nerves eat at my insides as I shield my breasts away as they try poking through the nightgown fabric. A furious blush erupts on my face as he watches my movements intensely.

Crowlen scoffs, pulling his heated eyes from my chest. "I need to make a few things clear." He begins to pace around the room. His movements make me squirm.

"Alright. Speak quickly and leave." I can't stand to have him linger in my safe space any longer than he must. His sinister presence forces my skin to crawl in the most lethal way.

Crowlen stops his bizarre pacing in the middle of the room. His red eyes capture my hazel ones. A smirk threatens to make its way onto his lips. There's something he's holding back. I bet he won't tell me a thing.

He clears his throat. The bobbing of his neck makes my insides twitch and heat flows down to my core, forcing my attention back into focus. I clench my thighs and hold my gaze more sternly.

"I don't want you near the king. Magic has wrecked his life enough. You added to the mix isn't what he needs." I have no clue as to what he's going on about.

"You act as if I know what you are referring to. I am not from Thrallen. Nothing that has happened in this kingdom is my fault. But he is now my king as well. I'll give my life to protect him and this kingdom. You can count on that." I mean every word.

That's the whole purpose of me being here. Why else would I become a knight? For the glory? I'm not like those people who hunt for fame. Never will be either.

Crowlen moves two steps closer. I freeze. His nose is very close to mine. Our breaths come together as one. This is insane.

"You'll wish you never walked through those damn woods. Dreaming of a glorious battle is simple. Having to live a bloody one is what you'll be getting soon." Crowlen bares his teeth at me. Making no mistake in his words. His sharp teeth shine from the many candles that have been lit around my room.

This doesn't explain his unspoken words.

"What are you keeping from me? What have I done to upset you so terribly?"

I truly don't care about his opinion of me. I hate that I'm being treated like a stupid child. If I'm meant to be fighting alongside him then we must hash out whatever the fuck it is that's got him so uptight.

He smiles wickedly, creating swirls of darkness tinged with deep red flames to fill the room. I cough due to the horrid taste that quickly consumes my mouth. Pained tears fill my eyes.

"I want you to understand that I will kill you if you decide to go after the king. I've met many women with magic over the years. Always claiming they want to make peace with a Madlock. But evil acts happen with each chance they get to grow close. I won't let you harm my king." Now I finally understand what this is about.

I speak with as much confidence as I can conjure at this moment. "You mistake me for a revenge-hungry witch. I cannot even light a candle without blowing out windows in the process. Believe me, my lack of control isn't worth the effort of being a murderer."

"No. You did move that piece of canopy three weeks ago.

166

You've got magic, powerful magic hidden inside you. I could feel it the moment you stepped into Thrallen. Your hair alone makes it obvious" Crowlen catches me off guard.

So, another person knows of my heritage. Why do people know more about me than I do? My father must have kept something from me to make both Crowlen and Artis squeamish. Hmm.

It was foolish of me to let my magic out to get a look at him. I back up to slump onto the bed.

Crowlen stays in his place watching each of my moves closely, waiting for me to strike. Well, I'm going to. He's shit out of luck.

"I won't ever use magic on King Kasper. It will go against everything that I've fought for in the Knight Trials. I give you my word. I'll prove myself to you if that's what it takes." Tears threaten to spill down my face.

That seems to give Crowlen another edge. He slowly stalks over to me. I reel in my pathetic pout. The warlock steps in between my legs, forcing his way too far into my personal space. The feel of his typical black leather breeches is enough to make my inner thighs beg for more contact. My exposed skin craves his inner fire. His hot body heat flows off of him in intoxicating waves. I shudder under his steaming gaze.

"Give me your hand." He orders me without any hesitation.

"Why?" A question that isn't going to be willingly answered by this complicated man. I'm more than skeptical of his hidden intentions.

He doesn't wait for more than a second before gripping my hand in his. His wicked touch is searing. I gasp as his fingers dig into my palms. Crowlen has a sense of authority that I'm tempted to rebel against. And yet I crave it. I hate him.

Crowlen slides his hand dangerously slowly up my forearm. His eyes trace over the blue veins that can be seen through my skin. He makes sure to travel over them with the tips of his fingers too. He maneuvers my hand to do the same for him. We hold onto each other's arms in a strangely intimate embrace. I've seen a few knights do this before. I think it's meant to be a touch of certainty and promise. And yet this is so very much more than that.

Suddenly an excruciating burn erupts through my skin. I lift to my feet in surprise, clashing against his not-so-surprisingly muscular chest. The tears I tried holding back now flood down my face and over my shaking lips. Oh, Seekers, my stomach is turning into the worst knots of my life. But then suddenly the pain stops and I can breathe again.

"What the hell was that?" I rip my arm away from Crowlen, cradling it to my chest, the back of my knees touching the bed again. My horrid sniffle echoes into the room and makes my chest jolt.

My eyes go wide at the sight of a baying crow newly branded in my skin by his magic. The red and slightly bloody mark resting in the middle of my inner left forearm almost glistens. I gasp from lightly grazing my fingers over the irritated skin. A shiver enters my spine.

"If you break your word I shall know about it." He motions for me to glance at his arm. Crowlen sports the same brand. The desire to claw his face off is extremely tempting.

The warlock practically tied my life to his. I've read about this in a book back in Coplina once. If I in fact harm a single hair on the king's head, then this mark will burn me even worse than before. He too will feel the same. Letting him know that I broke this sort of life promise.

Can I be any more damned for the underplace?

Crowlen doesn't wait for my protest or to demand that the branding must be removed at once. He and his quickly disappearing flames flee out of the room. Waves of raven hair flow as he harshly shuts the door behind him.

I sit here on the edge of the bed in total silence. Wondering what the hell just happened.

Being connected to this royal warlock with a vicious brand is not how I wanted to end my first day as a knight.

This little secret between us will surely kick me in the ass.

Twenty-Three

Sleep doesn't find me on this night. It might have been because of the constant cramping within my lady parts. Though the thought of Crowlen literally branding me with lethal magic is probably the main reason.

Just looking at my slowly healing arm gives me goosebumps.

Not even the desire for a brand-new day can ease any pain I'm experiencing. However, there are many more important things to worry about. I lay awake and try my best to keep still in the face of Thrallen.

After a while, the sun rises high in the sky. I get up quickly to dress in my armor. My battered sword is enclosed in its sheet. I even have this new shield with a beard molded in the middle. It feels heavy and right in my head.

To start good habits, I make the bed and head down the hall, descend the stairs, and meet my fellow knights where our king told us to be.

I watch as the town's people gather around the wooden stage in Celeste Square. King Kasper and his brooding warlock Crowlen gaze upon them all. Though his red eyes refuse to land on the knights. I wonder why.

Though I can't spot Artis and Kurty out of the corner of my eyes. I'm left feeling disappointed.

But then the announcing horns stop their deafening blows. The people grow silent. This means the king is ready to speak.

Kasper clears his throat.

"The queen of Pucnasia is out for my blood, our blood." I hear the shaking rasp in his voice.

"We will not let her bring down this kingdom over petty revenge. The Knights of Thrallen and I will march far to meet this queen. We will defeat her at any cost. No harm will come to you. That is a promise." The crowd of brave people cheer on the king. I watch him raise his fists in the air. A sign of his good words.

I suddenly want to make sure he upholds this promise. It's now my knightly duty to hold him accountable.

An hour passes me and the knights return to our room to make our final preparations. However, putting on my brown cape isn't as exciting as I want it to be. Having to mark my face to look like a man feels wrong. But I know I won't be able to change that. A woman as a knight is horrible in men's eyes. The very idea is barbaric. It might even be seen as an act of treason.

My true identity can never be revealed. That's a lie that I will have to learn to live with. At least until times change.

I braid my hair back as tightly as I can. It should fit underneath my helmet. Once I'm done, I head back down with other knights to get in our formation to leave the main city of Thrallen. We all look the same in our yellow tunics, brown capes, and shiny bronze armor.

We march out the front castle doors and into the streets. The people have been waiting for us. Most wait outside of the many cafes and shops with worry heavy in their eyes. I detest how this once happy town full of joyous laughter turned into gloomy frowns.

This impending battle is what causes all of this distress fueled by fear. I can feel the strained smiles of the people in the air. I sense their brewing sorrow on the tip of my fingers. My magic is called by it. I will it to borrow deeper inside of me until the time is right to truly call upon it.

The Knights of Thrallen are absolutely perfect in uniformity and strength. These men wouldn't be here if they didn't possess honorable strength. I barely made it through. I'll pull my own weight at any cost.

And yet it doesn't seem like it will be meant for anything. I'm starting to think that I'll be killed at the sound of the war drums. It's not a horrible idea. It happens to be a very reasonable inference.

I follow behind one man with simple straw-colored hair. His steps are long and quick. I can barely keep in step with him and the others.

I eventually find a few people hanging out in front of the Yellow Piggle. It's hard not to turn my head to fully gaze upon them.

I do hear Aunty Kurty cry out. She spots me in no time. Her voice says she wishes Anna, or rather Mason Triscan, luck on the journey into unknown dangers. My body wants to badly run to her side and sob into her motherly bosom.

No one can determine the outcome of this battle.

Dread consumes my guts as we finally start to march out the city gates. I see those familiar woods out in the distance. I remember fighting that magic vine with absolutely no skills whatsoever. My lips twitch upward after picturing that perfect hole in the tree where that strange creature lived. I even met the king within those sparkling trees. It seems to only have been yesterday, even though it was just three weeks ago.

How odd to think that I made it and am now a knight.

I see men gather in thick formations. Rows upon rows of chocolate brown capes fly in the chilled winds. Men of high ranking are making their rounds. Brutal generals lead the remaining knights into their stern troops. I spot Crowlen right down at the very end. He notices me too, perhaps feeling my heated eyes on his gloriously dark being.

It's honestly difficult not to drool over his appearance. Everyone else wears Thrallen colors while Crowlen is dressed in similar armor he wore during the last Knight Trial. But this set is heavy with power.

He's wrapped in a magnificent flowy dark red velvet cape that makes his gloomy purple armor seem to glow. The sparkles of the fabric shine in the high sun. His raven hair has been brought into a heavy thick braid falling to the middle of his back.

A few stray hairs blow against his face from the icy breeze. I gulp as a general with pale features guides me to Crowlen's small troop. I need to keep my twitching composure under control.

I make my way to the very back of the formation in a steady walk, trying my best to not trip over my own two feet. But it proves difficult with a cold stare hitting the back of my head. I need to hurry out of Crowlen's sight before I lose my nerve.

King Kasper waltzes down the lines of his trusted army, making sure all his men are ready to march ahead straight for danger. I make sure to stand straight as he hovers within my section. His eyes scan over me for a simple moment not knowing that I am a woman with an even bigger lie to stay hidden. Not once do I falter.

It's Crowlen's turn to examine us. He and the other generals double-check each man. Doing everything in their power to make everyone look their absolute best. It's when the dark warlock lands right in front of me that things become worse.

The warlock unfairly adjusts my cape. Making sure to grip the end of my hair tightly. I bit the inside of my cheek to contain a whimper. There's an unnecessary aggravated look plastered on his pale features. He's so close that I can pick out every little agonizing detail of him.

Seekers, he's beautiful. But aren't all wicked creatures?

His sharp teeth make my head spin. Crowlen is allowed to show off his power without any consequence. I'm lucky that my teeth have no prominent points or else I'd already have been arrested.

"My apologies." He says to me before moving on. Though not without jerking my shoulders first.

Very carefully, I shoot him a heated glare, hoping it will somehow cause his hair to burst into flames. Too bad this isn't going to be round two of our duel. Perhaps that makes me the lucky one.

The king makes his way to the center of the field at the very front of his men. His armor is completely gold. His cape is a pleasant lake blue color. His crown sits nicely upon his head. He has to stand out due to safety reasons. We need to be able to spot him in any situation so we can quickly get him to a safe and secluded location if necessary. Though his blue eyes are a nasty storm today. I don't blame him for being slightly moody.

He appears so bothered and squeamish in his stance. I don't like it one bit.

"I've made enough speeches today. You all know what must be done. Protect our kingdom and fight for peace. Let us march forth to our victory!" Kasper smiles like a young stable boy. As if he had no worries in the world.

I wonder if anyone else can see the evident fear in his young gaze.

And yet for some reason, I'm having difficulty wanting to fight for this kingdom. I know it's now my sworn duty. But I think I must fight for someone dear to my heart who is no longer walking on these lands.

The need to wield my blade to honor my father is what motivates my feet to move forward with the rest of the troop.

Twenty-Four

The Knights of Thrallen march in a glorious army for days and days.

I'm not exactly sure for how long. We only come to a stop at the latest hour when we're too exhausted to move on. The tents we have been provided by the generals are extremely small and only meant for a single knight to occupy. No lanterns are allowed to be inside of them with us due to threats waiting for a chance to attack from within the forests. The cold seeps in without any hesitation. I didn't realize that the temperature would drop so low the farther north we went.

It's like summer skipped over us entirely.

From what I know about Pucnasia, the monsters that call that kingdom their home have little to no weaknesses. I'm sure that the coming snow will not cause them any distress as it will for the Knights of Thrallen.

We knights are told to hurry and pack up once the first light crawls up from behind the thick trees. Our formation is much tighter than when we first started our journey. We're shoulder to shoulder, allowing our body heat to spread around us the best it can. My breath clouds in front of my face with each little gasp I take.

My legs are on fire, but I push on like the rest.

It becomes colder the farther into the deep wooden lands of Thrallen we tread. Snow eventually starts to fall on our helmets. My teeth chatter uncontrollably, causing my bottom jaw to ache. Those around me go still like a frozen lake, trying so hard to keep body heat intact.

Spring has blown away quickly during our travels. The shift in the season can be felt in the marrow of my bones.

A change so deep and sudden it's hard not to flinch from the sharp snap of it. Winter is already upon these lands. Mother Nature herself could not have shown up at a worse time.

But after taking a few glances at the other knights I can see that they can't feel the same. It must be due to the Seekers. Beings of the old magic who created Thrallen. Or who stopped the war before this land became Seekers Land. I'm still skeptical about them. I don't honestly believe seven ugly witches surfaced from the Lake of Souls to stop a deadly war. It seems too much like a fairytale.

Their heavily devoted followers would stop at least once a month in Coplina to preach their ways. I wouldn't give them the chance to visit me and my father's home as I chanced them away with a meat cleaver. I remember their blood-red cloaks flowing behind them as they ran. They want to be those witches so bad that I find it sad.

Maybe it's because I'm a magic wielder, a sorceress. Not just anyone can sense such things as me. There's no other explanation for it. It's the only thing that makes sense so far in this journey. Such powerful women are supposed to feel magic like this. It's buried inside my heart.

I'm only disappointed that I can't discover more about it.

I knew that the moment Crowlen sought out to hunt me. I still don't know of his intentions for me and I rather not find out either.

Now I march in a uniformed group of knights behind him. I wear a brave face. Anything to keep my sanity.

Though it feels utterly strange when I blush from the sneaky glances he makes. And yet they are meant to scare me into keeping silent. I hope no other person sees how red my cheeks get. An unknown emotion settles in my heart. There's no point in figuring it out now.

I probably won't live to sift through everything I might have felt once this battle commences.

The army that is Thrallen travels inside the dense forest that almost consumes the main part of the kingdom. The tallest trees I have ever seen. Massive spruces tower over everyone, doing their best to reach the height of mountains. The scent of the many pine trees creates a welcome sense of calm. I inhale deeply whenever I can.

The knights are forced to walk slowly. Dangers lurk all around us. I feel it all without any trouble. It's not only the sweet smell that alerts me but the crisp chirps sounding off occasionally.

As a child, I would read as many books as I could in the town's only bookshop. My mind was so intrigued with my father's stories that I just had to consume more. Whatever I could get my little hands on I'd devour with my eyes and mind. That was either Thrallen's common knowledge or books about magic. Texts inspired by magic were rather easy to find since Delvina allowed all people to live there with their powers.

A few books are stuck inside my memories like a plague. Ones of deadly magical creatures and what they prefer to eat. I never thought I would encounter such things. But all the signs are here now. The snow is home to them all.

Beasts with bodies of birds and heads of felines. Such different varieties that have been created as the perfect killers. Very stealthy creatures who crave human flesh. I know they crawl inside complex trees like these. They lure prey using comforting smells. Just like sweet honey for example. There is no name for them. No sure way to end their lives. Some have written a sharp sword decapitating them will work. That is if a hunter can get past their talons and fangs.

I keep a close eye on my troop. Making sure none of them glance into the trees for far too long. Me and the rest of the knights can't afford to lose anyone before arriving at the mountain valley. King Kasper gained fewer knights than he originally hoped for. We have to be careful.

Thrallen's army steps in complete silence. Not even our armor or bags of supplies make noises. It has to be a miracle. Pure luck we must have stumbled upon. If that is true then I'm certainly grateful.

But when a simple little twig snaps far off in the distance I immediately know we're about to be in a world of shit.

"Do not move." I hiss in a whisper.

The quietness of the forest allows my voice to carry on the icy winds. Some men glare at me with confused expressions. Others become still from sudden fear, afraid of what the fresh falling snow stirs awake. I manage to halt the whole army with my voice in seconds. I can't help but internally cringe as their eyes shoot to drag over me.

Maybe I should have kept my mouth shut.

"Just a noise. Nothing to worry over." One man standing to my left scoffs. This knight doesn't seem to think the silly sound is any indication of a threat. This angers me greatly. But he's not so excited to be stopped so suddenly. His muddy eyes are already red from the cold air hitting them constantly.

I don't favor the way he sounds. So arrogant. So oblivious to what's out there. I will let them all know.

I tilt my head. "None of us made that sound. Something is stalking us. Waiting for the perfect moment to strike."

A few others laugh around me. But there is one knight who keeps a worried expression. I see the chocolate hair of his poking out from his helm. Though from this angle I can't tell if his eyes are green or brown. However, I take his slightly encouraging expression as motivation to hold my ground amongst these men.

"You aren't serious, are you?" A man with terribly kept black hair and dark creamy skin questions me. Very humorous he is. His joking manner causes me to grow hot with anger.

But then the commander of the army shoves his way in between me and the knights. His white face twisted in annoyance. He doesn't have the time for a petty squabble. It's not hard to get in between the man and me.

He does make sure to keep his distance from me. Enough

space to make sure no one is uncomfortable. Huh? That's a first for him.

Maybe it's because Crowlen hates literally everyone except the king and doesn't want to touch a pesky knight.

You could say that the feeling is very mutual.

"What is this chatter about?" Crowlen does not really care for the conversation topic. He just needs us to stay silent. I guess that he too knows what I warned them about.

I grip his chainmail-covered arm, latching my fingers onto the iridescent purple arm cuff with a death hold. His red eyes shoot downward. That stare is already so intense. I somehow keep my cool and plead with my eyes.

Though I ignore the ticking of my heart. "You must lead us out of these woods. Bloodthirsty things are on the hunt for our flesh. Be a wise commander and don't get us killed before we even make it to the true battlefield."

Crowlen gazes upon me no longer and jerks his arm free of my grasp. He stomps ahead quickly. Does he even care about how much nose he's making right now? I bet all my gold and silver coin that he doesn't!

I fight the urge to run after him, to beg him to look around to find glowing green eyes shining out of the trees. I can feel them now. Watching these barely heated bodies mope around. I need them all to get away before it's too late.

"What is it Crowlen?" The king struts over to his warlock. A curious glint is in his eyes. I clench my fists tight, fighting that angry magic inside of me. Magic that is really no use right now.

The devilish man growls, it's a tickle to my eardrums. "Sir Mason believes we are being watched by creatures." He makes it sound as if I'm the crazy one.

181

If I get the chance, I'll show him crazy!

I struggle to keep my control. The desire to ram his pretty pale face into the nearest tree openly taunts me. I must stay calm. These men's lives might depend on my power. I hope it won't come to that. There's no guarantee I'll be able to wield it properly.

King Kasper snickers. "Of course, there are beasts of magic roaming in these forests. Sir Mason is right to be on edge. We must continue forward. The mountains are soon upon us."

His words take me by surprise. I didn't think Kasper knew anything of magic and all that follows it. Maybe there is more to him than being king and occasionally hunting for boar.

All the mighty Crowlen does is bow to his majesty and give me a nasty snarl while fully showing his teeth in warning. Then he calls upon his troop to go on with our journey.

Satisfaction lingers in my heart as we walk ahead.

Twenty-Five

I ce crystals trim my white lashes. Shaky white breaths fog
out before my mouth and from others. A tremble making
way into my chubby fingers. I'm glad to be a woman of
meaty bones. At least I'm not completely freezing like these
skinny men. It's a shame most of these men are tall and lean.
They offer no real fat to keep warm.

I'm extremely grateful to be a woman.

The army left the dense spruce trees hours ago. Harsh snow
makes it deadly to climb up slick hills. Everyone does their
best to shield themselves from the deadly flakes. Our glorious

capes are not helping very much against the powerful wind. A few coughs echo in the air. So far, this war is going terribly. And it hasn't yet begun.

I want to fall over and let the cold take me. But the sight of ginormous gray mountains with white tops changes my mind in an instant.

The Knights of Thrallen are brought to a stop before a monstrous valley. The generals line us all up to peer down into it. Gasps fill the openness. What waits down below is something out of a true nightmare. Not even I could have imagined all this.

Ugly blue giants sporting more than two eyes and terrifying yellow goblins cover every inch of that valley. I spot those creatures who call the spruce forests home. Every beast I read about resides down there. No true man in sight. This was very bad.

This can't be right, I think to myself. I'm not sure why I'm questioning the rumors of Queen Pearlina's kingdom suddenly. I know what her citizens are. Maybe it's fear that makes me doubt what's clearly right in front of me.

I glance around to see if anyone else has been surprised. There aren't any real shocked expressions like mine. Everyone already seems to be familiar with this monster army.

"What the fuck is this?" I ask out loud not expecting anyone to answer.

"The Queen of Pucnasia is no ruler of man. She craved a nasty monster's touch so terribly that her call had been answered by those very beasts you see. Magic within a woman's heart is evil and always will be." The same man who questioned me in the forest speaks into the air.

Though I don't get mad. I only grow more frightened of

what is to come. Dread fills my guts all the way to the top.

Tears build in my eyes, begging to be released. Devilish beings from bad dreams stand a few hundred feet away and make me want to vomit. I do just that right in the next available patch of snow.

I rest on my knees for a moment before the generals and commander begin their rounds. I finish puking up this morning's ration of bread and cheese until there is nothing left in me to heave.

Crowlen rushes to hoist me back onto my feet. I didn't know that he had gotten close enough to me. There is no protest within me. I don't have the heart to turn away from the warlock. He grasps my shoulders tightly, pushing me to the very back of the nervous army. The sight of monsters is quickly gone from my view. Temporary relief finds my frail soul.

He leans down to whisper in my ear. His heated breath kisses my chilled flesh. "Don't let this sight sway you from the knight's mission. Serve and protect the king. It's what you are meant to do."

Those soothing words are a dark fire in my chest. For a moment I think he might care. But then I hurry to shove the thought into the deepest part of my mind.

I pull away quickly. I even throw a few punches to his breastplate with brown-leather gloved fists, not caring about the bruises I'll have on my knuckles later. They won't matter. Tears slip down my face in steady streams. Anger bursts through my thick emotional shields. I can't stop everything that's running in me.

"How could you not warn me? I feel so much energy swarming around this place. It's eating me alive. The magic, it's too much!" I try my best to furiously rub the ache away in my chest, but this damn breastplate is in the way.

Mystical creatures, no matter how big or small, always have magic. Magic will be their advantage. Always. And I can feel it all, smell everything.

Crowlen looks around again. Making sure to not attract prying eyes. No one glances in our direction. The men are too busy watching the valley, scouting the best entryway. Their conversation is one of great importance.

"Ignore every damn excruciating feeling you got pooling inside you. You must not use magic against these beasts. It would ruin your cover and get you killed in an instant. Do this for me, Anna." Him saying my name gives me the most wicked of chills. Why is he telling me this?

I fight hard not to sob. I want to break down into fits of dramatic tears. But there's no time for such vulnerability. I need to get a grip on myself fast.

I stand straight and wipe the fresh salty tears away, adjust my twisted cape, and push a lone snow-colored strand of hair behind my ear.

A ghostly smile blossoms on my lips. "As you wish."

Twenty-Six

My eyes follow the king as he and his highest-ranked knights have a detailed discussion. Must be trying to determine which end of the valley we will enter. Though my mind is hovering over the big glamorous camp located within the monster army. A tent of rich green fabric is pitched with crystal spears. There's even a massive fire pit in front of it. That must be where the queen is hiding.

It doesn't take long for King Kasper to strut to the middle of his army. An army so much less than the one filled with goblins, giants, bird-cat beasts, and many more unnamable creatures.

Kasper clears his throat. The chilly weather has been making most of us sick. If I think about it too hard I might catch a cold myself.

"This petty war is because of a quarrel my father had with Queen Pearlina a long time ago. I know as much as you do. It was never my intention for us to meet like this. This battle will surely turn legendary after tonight." Kasper makes sure he's speaking to each one of us.

Like he's standing in front of every man personally. I don't like how this sounds. It makes it seem like many of these knights won't make it back to Thrallen or their families. That's a possibility I haven't taken a moment to think about. That encourages my stomach to twist again. However, I hold back anything left to rest in my stomach this time.

"A child never grew up because of their squabble. I intend to force this worthless feud to an end. Today and today only." He speaks in a confident tone that warms us all.

I have always wanted to know what knights fought for. Sure, the stories say for glory and pride, but I know it must be something more. Now I'm beginning to understand it all. Knights fight for what they believe to be true. Knights battle against great evil. Knights fight as one with grand honor and loyalty to the crown.

"We stand together strong and mighty. Don't ever forget who you are." Kasper raises his voice.

There is a pang of fear striking inside my chest. There is no way to avoid the feeling. I think I'll make sure to remember it's there so I can fight against it.

The generals and Crowlen face their troops with stern expressions. His soft red eyes have turned cold once again.

Crowlen uses a low tone this time. I truly loath it. It's not like the deadly warlock I've grown to know at all. "We march down the valley in mere minutes. Keep your heads up. Don't look back."

Me and the others drop our packs. My sheath is heavy with my battered sword. My boots are still stuffed with small knives. And my breastplate hides a machete as well.

I'm ready to fight this foe who threatens the safety of Thrallen. Winning my trials only proves there is a fight within me too.

"On my call, you will have a steady pace ten steps to your right," Crowlen shouts in a crisp voice.

A shake quickly ravishes my spine. Thrilling sensations worm their way into my guts. I bounce on my feet like an agitated toddler. I itch for this to begin.

Crowlen glances to the king for a signal. That's when I realize that my troop will be the first to enter the valley. Somehow, we migrated to the front of the army. How did I not notice this?

Kasper dips his chin. The signal. Crowlen grins, the corners of his lips form wrinkles around them. He's a menacing crow who loves to welcome danger at every turn.

"Move!" He yells at the top of his lungs.

Me and the other knights start a simple march. Then the edge of the cliff becomes a steep hill. We begin to sprint, forcing me to lift my feet a little high to keep up with the men around me.

This is it; I tell myself.

There is no way out of this. I never wanted a way out of my wildest dream. Not ever and not in a million years.

The first lines of my troop encounter the horde of beasts.

Screeches from the goblins fill my chilled ears. Without wanting to I watch as they claw into the stomachs of knights, men I participated in the Knight Trials with. It's such a sickening sight!

Giants move in to stomp on those they can easily catch. Flying cats with bird bodies swoop down and snatch knights away like it's nothing. Their terrified wails shake my soul.

Capes and ugly colored skin collide into a wave. Terror laces my heart. What am I going to do?

I retrieve my twisted sword once I find a place to stop for a moment to catch my fleeing breath. My irritated eyes watch the armies as they mash together into one massive blob.

But then an ear-splitting screech far too close for comfort shoots nervous through me. A goblin with foam at its mouth charges me. In a swift and yet twitchy motion I raise the weapon just in time.

"Shit!" I exclaim as the nasty thing falls in pieces at my feet. I sliced it into two parts. The blade slid through it like a mound of fresh butter.

I have no chance to recover from my first monster kill. It's the first of many to come my way in rapid waves.

A strange, blue-colored creature with pitch-black fangs and green hair sprints towards me next. I try aiming my sword at its chest, but it's too late. The beast grabs hold of my wrist. Its grip almost breaks my bones beneath my arm cuff.

"Hmm, such a pretty thing." It snarls in my ear somehow knowing I'm not a man. Maybe the creature can sniff out the difference in my blood. I cringe away. A gag flies out of my mouth. Its breath reeks of rotten fish, or maybe it's human. I rather not find out.

It's a miracle that I don't puke on its dirty ripped tunic.

I shift the sword into my free hand and whip it around hurriedly. The tip slices through its pointed ear. A sharp scream shoots from its mouth.

Thankfully, I free myself from its hold and run away before it can get me again. Though I'm almost trampled by a giant. It isn't watching where it's headed, mindlessly stepping about, narrowly avoiding a small group of knights who are fighting against two large orange trolls with thick green beards.

These things only desire to cause the most damage.

For hours and hours, I go up against the unimaginable. Even aiding other knights in fighting back a group of hilariously short but deadly goblins. I'm one of them now.

Death is everywhere I look. Human and monster alike. It's different from when I gazed upon my father's soulless body. He appeared peaceful as his spirit traveled to the heavens. It's this destruction around me and lifeless bodies that pain me greatly.

Never in my life have I wanted to prevent this from happening with my bare hands. I need to save the lives of my fellow knights as much as possible.

However, finding the king out in the middle of the battlefield facing a woman with pure white hair is a horrible shocker.

Without thinking I sprint into action in the direction of my king.

Twenty-Seven

K ing Kasper stands exactly as he should. Tall and full
of honor. Something this woman does not possess.
        I sense the darkness swelling around me. So
powerful that I may collapse. It's nothing I've ever felt before.
It might be worse than Crowlen's grim presence. That's got
to be deadly.

No other knight on the battlefield even glances their way.
All their attention is on the monsters that swarm this valley.
Most doing their best to make sure those horrid beasts step
no foot closer to their king.

I remain on the sidelines. Not really sure what I should do.

I step closer but stop instantly only a few feet away. The mystery woman twists her head in a crisp way. It distracts Kasper greatly. I shiver from the way this woman gazes at me. As if she can see past my helmet and blood-splattered armor.

Her eyes are the purest green. Flashes of yellow like a lightning bug flickering away. Yet they seem so familiar. So much like a knowing forest. But they're much colder and empty. This doesn't make any sense.

I study the woman with striking snow hair. The same pearly shade as the flakes that have paused their descent for the time being. She wears an extravagant gown made of deep green velvet. The fabric clings to her generous curves perfectly. I somehow feel insecure in my dirty and dented armor. Goblin blood has been smeared upon my blazing face. At this moment I'm not anywhere close to being pleasant to look at.

"Dear king, I think this silly battle has lasted long enough." I find it odd to hear the woman's voice.

I suddenly spot Crowlen sneaking around to get next to the king. He quickly jumps in front of Kasper, aiming his sword at the woman's throat. I almost shout his name in surprise but decide against it. This isn't the time to be a distraction.

The wicked woman grins madly. That chilled expression triggers a feeling inside me. One of remembrance.

Whatever this is, it isn't going to end well. Not by the way the queen looks upon Kasper.

Crowlen turns grim. "Crawl back into the filthy cave from which you came."

He doesn't hide his attitude. Seems like they've met each other before. Why does that make me sad? Everything is not starting to feel right.

I skip through grunting beasts and knights still fighting until they no longer have breath. My cape was ripped off of my shoulders long ago. It's somewhere hidden beneath the grueling snow now melted by the warm blood.

That makes it easier to wiggle my way past speeding yellow and pink trolls. Gross beings they all are. Fresh wounds and boils cover their reptile skin. Disgusting.

Trying to get a good spot to watch this dreadful interaction is tough. But I find the right place eventually.

The Queen of Pucnasia chuckles in a sinister tone. "That is no way to treat your superior." Her green eyes form into thin slits. Like a poisonous snake.

"You are no one to me," Crowlen growls in response.

Kasper gently pushes down his friend's arm, a sign for him to back down. The warlock is mighty hesitant but does so anyway. I see the tension floating around them three. I despise this woman already.

Queen Pearlina sighs before snapping her thin fingers. A cracking noise echoes off the high mountain walls. Massive loads of dust fill the snowy air in an instant. The colors of pink and blue blow around those who remain. No growls or screams float with the icy breeze. Not a nasty smell to be found. She caused her brutal army to simply vanish into nothing. They were toys to her. Just because she had the power to do so. Does she not realize that despite their wicked tendencies they are living creates? Being who also took breathes just like we do? Seekers, she's more evil than I could have ever imagined.

My freezing form wobbles. The small amount of power that Pearlina revealed made a whole mystical army disappear. There is no telling what else she might do.

The remaining Knights of Thrallen are in shock. There are

no more monsters to slay. Only broken and dead men remain.

"What was the point of all this meaningless destruction?" Kasper asks. Many small cuts freckle his flush skin.

I sense that his right knee is on fire. An odd trick I picked up as a child. Seeing an inflamed joint or twisted ankle is easy to spot for me.

Crowlen puffs his chest out like a bull toad in summer.

"Nothing is meaningless to me. I needed you to bring me my prize." Her blood-colored lips shift up. Her pearl-white teeth sparkle like untouched stone.

But I know this isn't for me to watch. I turn around to find nearby limping soldiers. An idea comes to mind rather fiercely.

"Help them back to the ridge. They'll need medical care. Find those who can clean and mend wounds. Go, quickly!" I search for every capable man who is strong and more than willing to help his fellow knights.

"Of course, Sir Mason." A man with long grey hair huffs after getting up off his knees. Must have been resting there. I almost feel bad about what I told him to do. Almost. He gives me a small bow and sets off on his order.

The man goes and tells others of this. They too move out to help those in need. I feel proud of these knights.

I begin to move to a knight who lies in a pile of dead goblins. The strong stench of their blood causes me to gag.

I attempt to help raise his head when a strong pull tugs at my waist.

I ignore it the best I can, doing everything to help him sit upright. My only worry is for my fellow knights. But the yanking turns worse. So powerful that I jerk backward in a jolt and allow the man to fall backward with a harsh thud.

My surprised shouts coat the air like an owl's hoot.

A magical tinge of sugar fills my mouth as I land in front of the queen. My armor clenches my ribcage which makes it hard to breathe for a moment. An extremely sweet taste that I never want to experience again.

King Kasper and Crowlen peer down at me. They're just as confused as I am.

"Excuse me. I've got men to help." My fake masculine voice slips up. I attempt to back away from the queen after getting on my aching feet. An invisible barrier blocks my way.

I lift my hand to try moving again and gasp in surprise. It feels like I'm touching pure glass that I can't see.

"What do you want with me?" I shuffle on my feet. Seeing her up close and personal is not what I imagined happening. So many features of Pearlina reminded me of someone I know. But who? What is going on here that I need to witness?

Pearlina stalks circles around me before she laughs. A real throaty grunt. "King Kasper, you are a fool. Can't even spot a witch when you see one." The queen's once giddy voice becomes sour. Much like her heart.

Kasper gazes upon me carefully. He doesn't understand. Crowlen knows exactly what the queen means. I wish I was anywhere else but here. Everything I have ever built for myself is going to be torn apart. It'll happen in a blink of an eye.

"What are you talking about, witch?" Kasper seethes. His short red-hot temper goes off. Even bares his royal blade to her, aiming right at her heavy chest. This makes the woman smile silly.

I still can't figure out why the queen needs to take revenge now. Her child was lost so long ago. Why not let her daughter rest in peace?

Pearlina scoffs. "You're blind within your own kingdom. If a woman like her can infiltrate the Knight Trials, then anyone can find ways into Thrallen."

I can't seem to breathe properly. My darkest secret is let out into the harsh world by this queen. A really devilish queen. Worse than Crowlen ever can be. I know that for a fact.

I'm absolutely torn. The look on the king's face is not one of fear. Pure anger sweeps across his features. Those ocean eyes now turn stormy.

Crowlen doesn't look much better. Though he has already suspected me from the beginning. Not much of a surprise for him then.

I clear my throat. A cry has been lodged at the very back of it. "I have no idea as to what you are speaking of."

I curse at the mighty queen with a few bruises on her white flesh. Maybe it isn't a good idea to play dumb with these people.

With one flick of the queen's hand, I'm being stripped of my armor and faded face makeup. My hair is no longer in that wondrous braid. I'm a bare woman in all their eyes. Just barely clothed in a perfect gown. A simple creation of the queen. Silky pink material wrapped around my full form, hugging my breasts tight enough to where they don't spill out over the sweetheart neckline. Still, my sheath and sword rest on my curved waist. Maybe left behind to mock me.

It's definitely doing its job to make me ever so stupid.

The king stumbles back in terror. It must be so disappointing for him. I hate how this came to be. It's the only way I was to be a knight.

Maybe if I explained from the beginning he might have understood. There is no going back to what could have been.

No hiding can be done now. I know this. So, there is nothing else to do but confess. I bring on my best brave face.

My father is present in my mind. The image of his soft eyes and thick gray mustache encourages me.

"I'm a woman who illegally participated in the Knight Trials. I'm a woman who faked Mason Triscan and his nobleman papers and his seal. I'm the woman who fought with my very soul in those trials. You must know that my king. I never meant to harm anyone." My voice is directed to King Kasper. His dark blue eyes are daggers in my vision.

Anything to help him understand is better than nothing. Though the queen's laugh irritates the underplace out of me. She's just so unnecessary to Thrallen in general.

"There is no law stating that a woman cannot become a knight." Crowlen pitches in. I shoot my eyes at him. Those red ones blazing away.

Why help me when I need everything but that?

Kasper rubs his face in frustration. "She lied about who she was. Created a false identity. That cannot go unpunished!" King Kasper declares whilst sneering at the queen.

"That was the only way!" My broken words fuel the disappointment inside of me. I move my gaze to stare at the snow beneath my feet. I realize that I'm still wearing my knight boots. I refuse to believe the risks I took to be where I am now were a mistake.

After a failed attempt to back away again, I'm pulled forward. This time I jerk away furiously as the queen reels in an invisible rope tightening around my waist.

Pearlina's wicked powers sizzle over my flesh like jittering butterflies.

I grow annoyed by this woman's petty magic. That sickly

sweet flavor turns old on my tongue. Something needs to be done. To damn what the king now thinks of Mason Triscan.

"You've revealed my secret. What else do you want from me?" My voice cracks from humiliation. I can't bear any of their stares. Shame fills me.

Queen Pearlina speaks very clearly. "That is not all that must be unleashed. I'm surprised there are no records of me being the royal mistress. Your father and I were lovers." She points a finger right at Kasper.

My eyes open wider. Crowlen's jaw drops slightly. This cannot be.

The queen continues on speaking.

"I believed us to be in love. I was wrong to think he would ever come to love a woman with magic. He really took great pity on me." I don't understand where this is going. Though I hear pain from the queen. However, it's not enough for me to want to comfort the bitch.

Pearlina paces, taking in the completely deserted battleground. No living knight is in sight. I was right to send them off. They should be safe far away from here.

The tall beautifully built woman sniffs back tears. "I tried convincing him to make me his wife and have magic legal for women again. He did not like either idea. Didn't desire me enough to get rid of that dreadful mother of yours. So, I took matters into my own hands to have my revenge." Her sneer surprises me. The queen's reaction to the mere sight of Kasper is puzzling, to say the least.

I desire to learn more. I must know why the queen's mission to take revenge is so important.

Crowlen's steady in front of the king. Blocking half his body in case the queen plans to attack. I'm left feeling lost. King

Kasper has nothing to do with his father's past. I'll make sure he doesn't pay for the late king's wrongdoings either.

I step away from Pearlina to gather a detailed picture of this bitter woman. Nasty power pours from her body. I vibrate with energy. I know Crowlen feels it within his bones too.

I decide to speak my mind about all this even if it isn't my place.

"What did you do to his father?" A sickening chill breezes through my hair. I shiver uncontrollably. It's the queen who lashes out in anger, causing the king and his warlock to crash down in a forceful heap. They land right on top of each other.

And yet somehow, I remain untouched. I wonder how that's going to last.

Pearlina smiles like a crocodile. Dark clouds circle the skies. Glorious winds swirl around. Vibrant pink magic consumes the air. That nasty sweet flavor makes me choke on my own spit. This doesn't look good at all.

Queen Pearlina speaks with horrible passion. It causes everyone to want to shrink down into ants. "I seduced the Madlock king. A child was then born months later. She did not die. An easy plot to start a war. To get my people back to the top of all." Shock is all that I feel. My eyes instantly land on the king.

Kasper appears unwell. His face turns a deadly shade of green. This news of an unknown sibling hurts him to the very core. His pain lingers in the air, it whispers to my heart, begging to be heard.

Utter rage fills my bones until they almost snap. No matter that the king's mad with me, I won't have this bitch upset him over something not involving him.

"And where is the child now?" Crowlen's tired of this

pointless conversation. I can understand that. He again lifts his sword. Prepared to cut off her head with one powerful slice.

I wish he would just do it already.

The queen huffs. Creating a dramatic tease. Making the warlock snarl with impatience. "She is here among us."

Her eyes wander over my shivering body. The cold has seeped into my flesh, and I can't seem to shake it. Pearlina grins in triumph.

At first, I didn't catch on to what she said. But it doesn't take long for the words to hit me with the help of her deep stare.

"You must be joking." A nervous chuckle escapes me.

Twenty-Eight

K asper shoots up to his feet in a rush. "That woman is no sister of mine."

He jabs a finger my way. No one can begin to imagine how sorry I feel for him. An imaginary fist punches me squarely in the chest. His quick denial brings me heartache. Though I can't find it in me to blame him.

I also refuse to believe a word from the queen's mouth. Crowlen's laugh indicates the same for him.

The sliver of a chance of more family already has evaporated into nothing. I'm not sure why I felt any hope at all even if it was for a split moment.

"Long story short, I gave away my child to some couple I picked off the road. They did not question me. Their only concern was for the innocent babe. So worried about the child going cold. I never imagined that my dearest offspring would unknowingly march right into my arms alongside the enemy. A perfect plan was then formed." Pearline claps her hands together in utter glee.

Hearing this confession forces me to my knees. I don't care about the wet snow seeping through the dress. Emotional pain explodes inside my chest. My breaths come and go in a hurry. Crowlen lurches forward but is stopped when Pearlina offers him a fierce stare.

The snow-filled winds are growing ever so strong. Making everyone's hair spin like tornados.

Kasper drops to his knees in defeat. So many things trouble his mind. I feel so horrible. I too didn't want any of this. This wasn't how anything was supposed to go.

This is impossible.

"I never was told where my magic comes from. I do know that my real mother loved me enough to keep me around. My father died believing I could be a Knight of Thrallen. That is what I did. No magic is involved. You are a liar, Pearlina." Denial perhaps isn't the best way to address this new issue. It makes no sense.

The queen doesn't seem to enjoy my outburst. "I am the one who carried you in my womb. I've come to take you home."

There is still something not being said.

"You've been watching me my entire life. Kept tabs on me within Thrallen. Then started an idiotic war just to get me back in your filthy hands. I would rather die than let you have me. I will serve my king. You are nothing to me." My words strike true in my heart.

It's strange that we have the same hair, similar noses, and perfectly matching brows. Now I can see why I look nothing like my dear father. This is just awful. Why didn't he say anything to me?

My entire life I knew I was different. But I never could have guessed that I wasn't his blood child.

Kasper has grown tired of the queen's talk. He steps forward out of Crowlen's hold.

"Fine. You used my father and created a bastard child. Now you will pay for putting my men in danger." Kasper raises his shining sword high in the air. Without thinking I do the same. The tips of the blades are so close to Pearlina's pale cheekbones.

I truly feel united with the king, my brother. He feels no anger towards me specifically. It's the fact that such a secret has been kept from us both that pisses him off.

The queen of Pucnasia twists her fingers. There isn't much thinking as I spring into action.

I shove out a hand towards the king. Kasper flies back by the force of a powerful wind. A wind created by my magic. The power that flows within my challenged soul. I'm more than glad it answered when I called upon it.

Adrenaline spikes inside me. The ground beneath my feet shakes. My magic has been almost completely blocked away for so long, refusing to release most of the time. I can't control how much I let out of my fingertips.

Crowlen rushes to his king. Long black hair flowing behind him.

I gasp sharply. I didn't mean to push him away so harshly.

The queen stares at me in wonder.

"You will not lay a finger on my king." The crow brand on my arm that I share with Crowlen burns hot. My skin sizzles as if it's being freshly marked again. I'll worry about the magical consequences later.

Pearlina doesn't care for my words. She only wishes to kill the last Madlock and start a new world. A world where women ruled over men. An exciting plan it is indeed. But not to me, her very defiant new daughter.

I pause and wait for the queen to make her next move. "You'd be wise to leave Thrallen. I don't want to hurt you." I tell her, ignoring the tremble of my voice.

Nerves eat me up from the inside. Confidence is no strong suit for me right now. But any words will have to do.

"As if a small girl like you could ever harm me. Come, child. We must be off." Pearlina offers her hand out to me. Her pale palm faces the pink clouds. Long black nails are at the end of her fingers. Not very pretty.

I make no move to take it. The thought of the queen's icy touch isn't appetizing. Bile rises at the back of my throat. I hold onto the sick. I desire nothing from this woman.

Truth be told, I'd rather die as an orphan than be taught magic by this terrible being.

"We will not tell you again. You better leave this place. Never come back to Thrallen." Crowlen moves to my side. We create a unified front. It must be a rather bizarre sight for us.

I dare to give him a pleased side-eye. I need support. At this point, I'll take whatever I can get from him. Facing a new mother is hard enough alone. Protecting the king should be our only priority. No one will harm him. Not ever if I have anything to say about it.

"You can't even light a candle without letting out too much power. What makes you think I won't kill you and this useless warlock?" Pearlina chuckles. Her crisp white brows rise to her hairline.

I offer her a wicked smile. "Because you need my magic. I'll never give it to you. I am Anna Scarrow. No man or witch shall take it from me." Something inside of me swirls madly. It's my magic finally getting in tune with me. I've waited so long for this day to come.

Standing up to this bully is no different than escaping jabs from those fellow knights.

Pearlina's no different than a man hungry for power. I don't care enough to want to rule all over women to make them more powerful than men. It's not a smart way to win. The queen only wants all magic to herself. I'm not going to let that come to pass.

"I've had enough of this. Time to die, daughter." Pearlina summons a wave of snow that sends the warlock soaring backward. Leaving me vulnerable against this true witch.

"Kill me then. Destroy your greatest weapon." I'm a smart girl for the most part. It should be easy to get underneath Pearlina's skin. I managed to do it to Crowlen with ease. This queen is no different.

The older woman smirks. "You are nothing to me."

I know better. I always can tell when someone lies. It was not a witch perk. I gained that power from my father. Ceden Scarrow.

"I am everything you ever wanted to be. I am power." I've never bluffed so badly before in my life. A silly thing to say.

It works like a charm too.

Twenty-Nine

I jump as a bolt of pink lightning erupts from Pearlina's hands. The energy scrapes against my side. Painful jolts pulsated throughout my being.

This is the third time that I've been struck in the same spot. I'm not going to be surprised if I make it out alive with my entire side covered in black and blue bruises.

A cry escapes me as I land on my knees. My shaky hands press against my bleeding side instantly.

"You are no match for me." Pearlina snarls. She then chants a few mystical words to unleash another horror upon me.

Terrifying twists of black glittering smoke surround me so harshly that I accidentally inhale some of it. It scratches the insides of my throat. The dark sparkly cloud backs me into the middle of the queen's blazing stare. For some reason it creates some sort of protective barrier. Or maybe it's a wall. I guess the difference doesn't matter.

I say through gritted teeth, "You don't know a fucking thing about me, *mother!*"

Well, that felt incredible.

I spit out the loose title with as much venom as I can muster. It strikes a nerve in the queen. I see agitation bloom across her serpent eyes.

I rise up off the ground slowly, hands shaking wildly. I crack my knuckles. A wild split echoes in the air. Allowing my magic to flow freely. I'm not going to hide it. Not ever again.

The ground trembles. Pearlina looks around in wonder. Trying to figure out what is going to happen.

I've read books with simple spells and tricks. I'll put them to the test here, now.

A tether of magic slips away. It branches into a thousand phantom hands. Touching as many rocks and boulders as possible.

The only real challenge now is to lift them off the ground.

I tug with my heart. These rocks grumble with extreme passion. I struggle to make them all float in unison. A nasty pull is settling within my fingertips. I use my hands to guide them higher into the air.

Pearlina stares with surprised eyes. Like a dumb pigeon watching two cats fighting in an empty street.

I spy Crowlen slowly creep up behind Queen Pearlina. I don't make my stare obvious.

But then I jerk my whole body back. I somehow managed to break through the black glitter barrier. I fall out of the smoke corral. The rocks mimic my movements, flying away from me and slamming into the queen roughly.

Pearlina cries out. Blood streaks down her eerie face. I feel no pity.

"You foolish child." She snarls. The queen forms her own boulders. But they are literally created from matter that Pearlina has manipulated. Something I will never be able to do. Not yet at least.

I hurry to roll across the ground. A massive rock almost collides with my skull. It's a kill shot that misses its mark by mere inches. It angers me. I know lust for purpose. This queen will not take my knighthood. No one will. Over my very dead body.

~ ~ ~

We fight long and hard. It feels like hours have passed. A few knights traveled to the ledge of the valley. They watch magic be tossed from one to another. I can feel their curious gazes on me.

Their eyes are wide with fear and others from excitement.

It must be strange seeing Sir Mason use magic. They can't attempt to question it. This battle is meant for us and us alone.

Both the queen and I throw everything we have at each other. I'm absolutely drained. There is that spark within me that won't stay lit. I need a boost of some kind. Though I won't be getting one anytime soon.

Pearlina isn't even breaking a sweat. She's fucking insane!

She watches me wither from tiredness. It brings her great

joy to watch me suffer. She wants to take my magic and destroy Thrallen with it. Fuck that.

"You bore me greatly. Sad to see so much potential go to waste." The queen pities me.

I suddenly have a great desire for this queen to piss off. I'm too tired to talk anymore.

The use of my magic is too much, too powerful. Draining my body of all the energy I have left. I've cast so much at once. Never once had the chance to.

This queen wants me to beg for my life. I will not. A knight does not beg a witch. I won't succumb to this queen's power. Not ever.

Pearlina keeps talking about nonsense. Pacing around. Waving thin arms in the air to form dramatics. Going on about her massive plans for Thrallen. How she'll rebuild the castle into one massive ballroom. Or what she wants to do to the courtyards.

No one wants to hear her speak any longer.

Crowlen hovers behind a moved boulder. Occasionally poking out his head. Trying to pick out Queen Pearlina's vulnerable spots. He sees none. It makes him curse out in frustration.

He knows that it's all up to me. I can see the worry in his red eyes. A warlock like him should be scared. Me and the queen are about to cast our final spells.

"Let us finish this, queen bitch." I shout and conjure green flames. The soft warmth flashes against my open palms. Such a soothing feeling. Like I can have it curled around my soul for all eternity and reside in a peaceful slumber

Pearlina stops her annoying talk to watch me raise my blazing hands. Now I know how Crowlen feels when he wields

210

his wild red flames. It's more than exhilarating.

Ever so gently, I push my fingers forward. The queen throws out her own sickly pink fire. The two magics come together but don't mix. Glorious lights slip away from the collision, entering the newly darkened skies above us, illuminating the clouds like brightly colored stars.

Each power is different. Mine is filled with extreme vibrancy, pureness, and love. Representing my internal strengths. I read somewhere that green is a symbol of light. At least according to Seekers text.

Savage pink is what the queen bears. No light magic is inside her heart. It's been obvious since the beginning.

I push my fire the best I can. But the queen is unfortunately stronger. The lighter-colored flame pulsates toward me. I step wrong and twist my ankle. A thunderous crack screams from my fractured bone. I grit my teeth in an effort not to cry.

Pearlina cackles like an old woman. Her grass-colored eyes spark with pleasure.

I shove out another hand trying to conjure more green magic. Nothing seems to be working. The queen only needs to use one hand.

Suddenly the warlock leaps from atop the rock, attempting to tackle the queen. She seems to have seen this coming. Queen Pearlina moves her pointer finger at Crowlen. He has no choice but to use his own darkness as a last defense.

I taste his foul power struggle against the queen's hovering hold. It's a flavor I welcome. Mixing my cinnamon tinge with Pearlina's gross taste of evil sweetness isn't wanted at all.

She keeps Crowlen afloat in the icy air. His hair blows across his tense face. Damnit, I can't do anything to help. I think I'm losing feeling in my hands.

The queen howls and snorts. Tearing her eyes back and forth between me and the warlock.

"You both are pathetic." The queen claims.

That is my last straw.

I feel seething anger flood my withering body. That thing that always lingers within my soul finally letting loose. Crowlen senses it slither inside me. His eyes instantly watch me stand.

My once hazel eyes melt into a forbidden green. As bright as a spruce tree. Their glow is so unreal. I don't stop the old magic that brews in my flesh and bones. Magic that only the Seekers are rumored to wield.

Pearlina watches in horror as I hover in the low skies.

I don't dare stop the sinister smile from forming on my lips. This is me accepting what I am. A magic wielder with power most can only ever dream of having.

I summon this grand magic to fuel my present flames. The green fire quickly consumes Pearlina's. The evil witch is now covered in the terrifying green that I created.

The queen's screams fill the air. Such an unnatural sight. Even her hold on the great warlock is no more. Crowlen crashes to the ground. I follow right after him.

Whatever sudden source of unmatched power I held is gone. I too rush into a heap right next to King Kasper. I make no move. My eyes flutter shut, clenching together tightly.

The Queen of Pucnasia is at last defeated.

And yet I'm left destroyed. Something darker than sleep drags me deep into my mind. I sense Crowlen running to my side right before I lose myself to this darkness.

Thirty

Crowlen

"**D**on't you dare die here, Anna Scarrow." I let out an involuntary cry as I cradle her limp head atop my dirty lap. Not caring a bit about the nasty goblin blood lathered in her white hair. There's barely a breath inside her fruitful lungs. Her once rosy cheeks have gone white as her hair and the small number of freckles on her cheeks and pretty nose disappear.

Dread and pure agony fill my heart rapidly.

I scan her blank face. There is no more life within her. And that's the most terrifying thing I've ever had to feel in my entire life.

A few decades of being on this plane could not have prepared me for a loss such as Anna. I'm not ready to let this aggravating woman go. I must do something!

"What has happened?" My king asks in a groggy tone. He awoke from his simple slumber. Anna knocked him away so hard to the ground that he fell unconscious. Good thing he witnessed nothing. Heard nothing of her magic.

I release a trembling breath. "Thank the Seekers you're alive," I tell my greatest friend Kasper. There's an obvious shake in my tone. I don't bother to hide it.

Though my gaze refuses to leave Anna. This is my fault. I'm responsible for all of this. If I hadn't been so stubborn and actually trained her none of this would have happened. It's too late to ponder on what could have been.

My thoughts of killing her consumed my mind every time we were in each other's presence. I feel unnaturally sick. Had I been wrong for my vicious ideas of slitting her throat? Why am I experiencing remorse now out of all times?

The king twists around. The sight of a dead Anna makes his heart grow cold. Not even the chilled air can be compared.

He joins me. His fingers find her wrist. Though I know there's no pulse. "She isn't with us, my friend," Kasper announces.

Sadness fills his tone. King Kasper barely has any regrets in his young life. But now I believe he wishes to have known Anna. Mason Triscan was a mask for her. Now neither live to explain their truth.

A big tragedy all this is. Something horrid happened on

these battlefields. Those who peer into the valley have no fucking clue as to what has occurred. They watch in grand confusion. Their minds are hungry to get a taste of what has gone on. Nothing is making any sense to them.

Well, they better get the fuck in line. I don't give two shits as to how they're feeling.

I'm so distraught and angry. I never wanted to actually kill her. Not even when I hunted for a witch in Thrallen.

Anna was different. Magic was not the reason she lived. I might have learned something from this strange woman. If only I didn't act selfishly.

"We must bring her back. The knights will want a proper burial for her." Kasper attempts to tug me away from her. My shoulders jerk away from his touch.

I will not accept this. She doesn't deserve to be gone. Something must be done.

With trembling legs, I stand on my feet. I peer down at her empty body with longing. And to think that I watched her for weeks, always around the corner wherever she was. I witnessed the people of the city get to know her. I rather enjoyed how the children welcomed her into the little games. Seeing her fight in the trials made me feel something, it might have been liberation.

Anna always went up against me with full force. She was never afraid of what I was capable of. Because she was just like me. Only I could openly use my gift of magic. Her rights had been taken away decades before.

I never realized how unfair it all is until now.

I tilt my neck. Cracks from my spine rattle the air. Kasper watches me with great suspicion.

"Whatever you plan to do, don't. It is not worth upsetting

215

the natural balance of this world." My king warns me.

The many years spent with me taught Kasper many things. One is that I have no impulse control.

I rip away at my breastplate. The armor piece descends to the ground and creates a thump. Next goes my tattered cape. I don't care about anything now. Only the thought of a smiling Anna beams in my frazzled mind.

Getting back down on the ground is the easy part. My knees force dents in the brutal snow. This empty feeling inside of me is wrong. That blazing fire that caresses my soul has finally been doused in chilly stream water.

That water being the death of Anna Scarrow.

I grip Anna by her limp shoulders tightly. Then, I bring her into my chest rather hungrily. Treacherous tears stream down my face. Being vulnerable isn't normal for me. I can't figure out why I cry for her.

This is a mess that can't be explained.

King Kasper has never seen me shed one tear. Watching me now must be troublesome. Having to hear me sob is heartbreaking. The king silently mourns with me farther off to the side. The sister he never knew existed is cold and dead.

Suddenly, I crave to know everything about her. I bet Kasper never felt so stupid as he does now.

There is a voice inside of my chest that encourages me to let out the darkness. I carefully press a hand against her plump chest and inhale her scent deeply. I start to chant a familiar language. Just whispers of Seekers prayer.

Kasper hovers in silence. He doesn't want to disturb me. Good. The king slowly drifts away back to his depleted army when he realizes that he can't talk me out of this. Perhaps he thinks I'm giving her a blessing. It's not too far from the truth.

My mystical words grow louder with the soaring winds. Mine and her hair spin greatly together, connecting like two halves. This dangerous spell I thought of is the only way to bring Anna back.

It seems to be working. In an instant, I feel my very soul split in two. With a furious growl, I search within her body. Trying to find any ounce of magic that's left.

But then my mental tether runs into a thread of life inside Anna. I latch onto it, pushing half my soul through Anna's heart. I feel it bind to her permanently.

It is done. She will live again. But magic always comes with a price.

Thirty-One

O nce a new icy breath settles in my lungs I spring forward, suddenly wide awake with my body aching all over. I take the first exhale of a rebirthed life. I am different inside and out. New and old magic lingers within me. And yet somehow beneath this buzzing charge that offers interesting emotions I still feel the same. I am me. I'm Anna Scarrow, Knight of Thrallen.

Lean arms draw me against a tough chest tightly. My face is being squished against very hard muscles.

"What's going on?" I can't believe those are the first words to come out of my mouth the moment I regain consciousness.

The only thing I really remember was feeling epic. I killed the queen. Ended her race to vengeance. What happened to me? No answers are coming to mind.

"You died killing that evil witch who had the nerve to call herself a queen." Crowlen sniffles in my unruly hair, his voice hoarse from harshly crying.

I died? Seekers, I died using all that magic in one go? At least now I know what not to do.

After peering up at him from under his chin I can see he's a miserable mess. His ruined eyes lock with mine. I pull back more to gaze upon his glistening face, taking in his twisted lips and furrowed brows. Without too much thought I bring my sore pointer finger to wipe away his remaining tears. They're so cold. I can't help but shiver.

I feel pain from his odd behavior. The sight doesn't sit right with me. I want to fix whatever it is that has made him so upset. Crowlen peers down at me with red eyes that turned puffy. Somehow, I can sense the change in my own.

He did something truly dangerous. I think I know what. But the thought alone threatens my sanity. I feel whatever he did to bring me back deep inside my chest, my soul.

And just like that it becomes real. Many of the books I've read always warn magic wielders to stay away from old soul magic. It appears Crowlen did everything in his power to ignore it. Typical of him.

By giving me half his soul to live I will forever have this constant reminder. My right eye now Crowlen's bright crimson. And the left remains my rich hazel.

"You had the chance to make me stay dead. What changed?" It's a fair question to be asked. I thought he was determined to kill me for my magic. And yet here I am in his ruthless arms and very much breathing.

This is the first time I've ever seen him smile. Truly smile. It's the most beautiful expression. Seekers, he's gorgeous even with those sharp fangs. This is perfect.

"I'll explain everything in time. Let us get you back to Thrallen, my knight." He tells me while fighting more tears away. I'm glad that he isn't trying to hide this side of him from me. I enjoy him like this.

After a few moments, he helps me back to my feet. I don't feel dizzy or anything. But I am left feeling slightly exposed in this torn dress Pearlina made me wear. Me and Crowlen climb out of the valley. My battered sword and Thrallen shield have been lost on the battleground. I'll have to find replacements for them if I'm granted permission to remain a knight.

We are greeted by the rest of King Kasper's army. My heart sinks at the shockingly low number. Crowlen doesn't seem to mind me gripping his arm to hold myself steady. In fact, by the way he's smirking, I can guess he enjoys my touch. How odd.

The coldness within him carefully balances out the heat coursing inside of my being. I think I'm starting to crave it.

Many shocked faces glance our way once entering the newly formed camp set at the edge of the valley. Their eyes are picking us apart. I unknowingly dig my fingers into his tunic sleeve. His lips attempt to tug upward.

But there is something that I must do to clear the air. I need to find Kasper. There are so many words I wish to speak.

Crowlen senses this.

It doesn't take me long to spot King Kasper binding a knight's leg up. I see that his facial cuts are starting to scab over. I thank the Seekers for this. Though I'm sure Crowlen is the source of his rapid healing.

The funny joke he tells is meant to cheer up the injured man. However, it's not working in his favor. But his work stops when his patient turns to gaze upon the new arrivals. The king places down the medical supplies to follow the knight's line of vision.

Shock fuels his features. I suddenly wish that I can simply disappear. Nerves eat at my insides.

King Kasper instantly rises to his feet. A borrowed cape he must have snagged after he reached the top of the valley falls to the snowy ground. His jaw goes slack in awe. Maybe it's the realization that the first woman knight is living once again. Or that his warlock is attached to my side as if his life depends on it.

"How?" That is all that he asks.

There really is nothing else to question. This is all that matters to him. I feel his concern and disbelief a mile away. I need to tell him so much. The urge to get to know him as my family slowly bubbles within my strained heart.

I step forward. My eyes meet his ocean ones. I search his face, looking for any sign of anger. There is none to be found. Only guilt and self-pity are what I can see. He shouldn't blame himself.

Crowlen eases me away from him slightly only to grasp my scraped hand in his cold one. I soak in the feeling. Like it's meant to have happened all along. It just needed a little push. A force so powerful that we would finally come together.

I draw in a deep breath and speak with all my womanly might. "How matters not, my king. I am here for a purpose. Let me fulfill my destiny."

221

Thirty-Two

T he long journey back to Thrallen is rather difficult. The harsh winter does not cut the army any slack. Some don't make it to the woods bordering the walls of the center city of the kingdom. Their deaths are quick and full of the cold. Kasper demanded that the dead be buried within the sacred cemetery. No one dares to suggest something else. We do just that as soon as we arrive back in the main town.

Sorrow fills our chilled bones while we dig in the dirt with our bare hands and swords. Kasper utters a simple prayer meant to honor the fallen knights and ask the Seekers to grant them safe passage to the heavens. None of us arrive in Thrallen in a good mood.

Crowlen suggested that I travel by his side. The excuse he came up with made me skeptical. He claimed that since they know now of my true identity some might do things. I truly doubt that the knights will cause me harm.

It would go against the code we hold dear to our hearts.

Most praise me for my bravery. Others only ask innocent questions. My way in the Knight Trials makes them all curious. So, I tell them how I did it. I don't bother to hide the details.

I assure the warlock that I'll be fine marching in our remaining troop. That doesn't give Crowlen peace of mind. He groans every time a knight sneaks a glance at me. Almost as if he's jealous of their boldness. I don't have it in me to tell him that he has nothing to worry about.

I catch him glaring at a few. The ones who lean in to hear my words better. Though I don't understand what the problem is. It's just innocent talk between fellow knights. What's the harm in that?

Soon we reach the massive gates. It's not long before we are spotted. Guards atop the lookout towers yell out for the doors to be opened. Crowlen's enchantment on the big doors work like they did that first day I arrived. His darkness consumes my lungs. Having half his soul gives me some emotional access to his power whilst it's in use. It offers me the strangest chills.

Thrallen's mighty army marches inside with victorious faces. Or at least some try to have those. Most of us are tired and sad about the many losses. Not a very exciting homecoming.

I just want to see Artis and Aunty Kurty already and eat her famous rabbit stew.

Besides my new brother and Crowlen, these people are my family. I wonder if they thought me to be one of those who died on the battlefield. Who knows what the city and outlining villages have heard during our journey.

Everyone gathers in Celeste Square. The army takes a stand around the stage. Our formation is crisp and true. I'm placed at the very back away from nosey eyes. King Kasper will have a word with me in the morning. No need to get on his bad side now.

Crowlen is next to the king. His eyes sometimes wander over in my direction. I refuse to offer the same gaze. My heart is too heavy with fear of what might come of my stay in Thrallen.

"My grand people. The battle against Pucnasia is fought and won." Kasper speaks loudly. The whole town cheers greatly. The knights shout their code. I do not participate. I'm not a knight anymore due to me breaking this very code. Keeping secrets gets people killed.

The king carries on. "Many good men lost their lives. A memorial will be given at the cemetery at first light by the knights. Please, those who have lost loved ones should attend. Thank you all for staying brave. Rest easy this night."

Everyone files away to their homes and taverns to either celebrate this slight win or drown their sorrow in mead. The knights have been ordered to their rooms. I linger around for a while, watching the wounded be carried away to the court physician. I don't dare to go back inside the grand castle.

My feet eventually lead me to the Yellow Piggle. My precious mentors are already waiting inside. Artis sees me first. The big man rushes towards me. His meaty arms circle around me with no hesitation.

"I've missed you too." I barely mumble into his chest.

Suddenly I'm being pulled into Kurty's hold. And that's when I truly break apart. I fall into harsh sobs. My tears seep into her shoulder, snot trails down my red face.

The brand of a crow in flight still throbs on my arm. I don't doubt that Crowlen can feel my pain. Our new connection will let anything slip away. There is a small nudge at the back of my chest. I think that's his way of letting me know that I'm not alone in my secret anymore. That I won't have to suffer in silence. Is that supposed to help?

"You won't believe what I had to do out there. What I let my magic do." My voice crackles.

Kurty leans back and plants a comforting kiss on my hair. Somehow it makes me feel worse.

"Tell us everything at your own pace," Artis says. He doesn't want to overwhelm me.

And that's what I do. I explain Pearlina's plot to seek revenge which really wasn't revenge at all now that I think about it. How that raging woman was my mother and that makes me her bastard child. Telling them that she wanted me for my power and that I stopped her.

I cry about the queen revealing my true identity to the king. I was lucky that Kasper didn't witness me use magic. He would have killed me where I stood. Or at least I thought he would in that moment. I'm not so sure now. It's hard to tell.

Artis grips a chair tightly. He wants that witch to pay. Kurty can't think of anything to say or do. The news is so tragic. It takes her words away.

I feel drained of everything.

"Crowlen brought me back from the dead. I share his very soul." Somehow that makes me cry harder.

I don't understand why he did it. He doesn't bother to tell me anything he is thinking. It's selfish on his part. Keeping the reason away has been torture for me. I will get it out of him soon. He can count on it.

~ ~ ~

I walk back to the castle slowly due to my not wanting to rush the night. I'm a broken spirit as I drift through the courtyard. It's a surprise to see the various roses and other flowers still alive beneath the loose snow. I take a seat before the water fountain. It's beautiful, especially the frozen water that is still lingering about down the spout.

The sound of the night birds is somewhat soothing. Scents of different flowers flow into my nose. The rich grass that's still alive coats my senses. It feels like being back in my old village. The only person missing is my sweet father.

More tears spill down my face. I don't care that they soak my ripped bloody tunic that I found lying around on the valley edge. It did the job of covering me while a knight helped me find a spare pair of pants. My shirt is so dirty that it's now a muddy orange color. I wipe the snot off my nose with my sleeve.

Nothing matters anymore. It terrifies me to think that I might feel this way forever. Shall it ever go away?

The need to give up on everything that I've worked so hard for is hitting me hard. The idea of running away and never returning to Thrallen creeps into my mind. This doubt, this self-pity, is a disease that I never wanted. It'll rip me apart if I let it.

But it flies away as someone in a dark cloak enters the

courtyard.

"I'm sorry, I was just leaving." I quickly stand and wipe my face clean.

The person makes no sound as I begin walking out the gates.

"You don't have to leave," Crowlen utters in a whisper. Or as nicely as his deep voice allows him to speak.

I pause in my tracks. Heat rushes to my face, making me a blazing fire. Very slowly, I turn to him. There is hesitation hidden in my aching movements.

His eyes are already dragging over me. Trying to find any physical thing wrong with me. Once he finds nothing odd Crowlen sighs and takes a seat where I once sat at. My heart thumps wickedly at the sight of the muscle in his jaw clenching.

I take this new silence as an invitation to sit next to him. My body tingles from his brooding magic. It sings to my own. I'm drawn to him whether I like it or not. The half of his soul does its best to intertwine with mine. But there is something there blocking that from happening. I can't decide if I should be grateful or not.

"Why did you save me?" It's a question I keep asking myself. This time I want it to be answered. I'm tired of dragging it out. Better ask now before he runs away with his tail between his lean legs.

Crowlen tilts his head. "You needed to live. I was the only one powerful enough to do the spell. That must be a good enough answer for you." He makes it sound so simple.

I can't stand it!

I scoff. "Splitting your soul to place in me was the only option? I find that hard to believe."

Crowlen leans to whisper in my ear. His loose black hair tickles my neck. Seekers, why does he do this to me?

"There was no other way." It compels my skin to crawl from the way his hot breath fans across me. I gulp down, squishing my thighs to stifle the bundle of nerves between my legs that hum from this. I hate it. But do I still hate him?

My eyes flicker back and forth from his lips and brutal red orbs. Has he always had such thin lips that look so inviting? I shake my head to get rid of these intrusive thoughts.

"You could have just left me for dead. Crowlen, you chose to rip your soul to bring me back. I-I think you have grown fond of me. I can say the same for you, unfortunately." Somehow in his presence, I am bold. These emotions flowing within me are giving me this courage. I wish I could thank them.

Crowlen is no mere boy. He's a powerful man with the darkest magic. Such powers were given to me. He must not have thought of how his magic bonded with mine. I can still feel it course through my bones. A burden I now share with Crowlen. Though I wonder how much he will allow me to sense.

Maybe I won't think about it like that after a while.

He comes even closer. Dark hair graces my upper body. Draping over me like a thick raven-colored curtain. Trapping in the warmth from our mingling breaths.

Crowlen is a man of many things. Romance is not one of them. But he seems as though he pictures me as a tall, chilled drink of ale on a hot day. It's the same feeling for me. Truly new indeed. Never have I experienced such things for anyone. Why does it have to be this warlock?

Tingles spread across my face. Blush making its way up my neck. If I didn't know any better, Crowlen sports the same red cheeks. The lantern light lining the courtyard walls gives away his visible reactions.

I want to laugh at his failed attempt at looking like he did the first day we met. All brooding and unbothered by everything in his presence. I don't think I'll be able to see him as a brutal warlock any more.

"You can call it fondness?" He laughs under his breath.

Was that the wrong word to describe what this feeling is inside of me?

"I think it is called attraction. You are a glorious woman with power that even I'm having a hard time comprehending. You, Anna Scarrow, are the light that suddenly appeared in my never ending darkness." Crowlen just keeps on surprising me.

It will always be an unexpected conversation with him. I like the sound of that. With an open heart, I take these sacred words and brand them to the inside of my heart. I hope they will forever bring me comfort as I recall them.

I smile as if I am a shy village girl who just caught the eye of my crush. The warlock returns one with the same force. It's a brilliant look on Crowlen.

"Alright, dark and gloomy warlock. What shall happen now?" I ask while staring off into the distance.

Taking in the night sky full of stars. My peculiar sarcasm laced those perfect words. Crowlen seems to be enjoying my annoying tone. As if he waited to hear me talk for his whole life. I share the same feeling.

Crowlen carefully takes my hands in his. My pale skin is nothing compared to his. He's a ghostly shade that causes me to shudder. This warlock emits such a cold energy that I have to suppress a shiver. I'm beginning to crave his flesh upon mine. And yet I'm surprised that his skin isn't smooth. There are callouses on his palms and some of the pads of his fingers. The roughness of them causes my chest to seize.

I shift my gaze to him and give his hands a squeeze. Crowlen is so close to me. Our noses barely touch. Our breaths become one.

I let out a small sigh as he carefully tears away from me. He creates an excruciating distance between us. Though I have the feeling that it won't last long.

"Well, She Knight...I suggest we prepare you for your first family affair. It should be a very entertaining show."

Epilogue

I stand in front of the occupied throne. I'm wearing no Thrallen armor, only the clothes and packs I arrived in the kingdom with. Dry soil and sweat still cover my entire being. That's no concern of mine now.

King Kasper gazes down upon me with such confliction that I fear he might topple over. I see his brutal inner battle within his stare. I can't do anything to sway his mind. Whatever decision he made is final and I plan to accept it with all my heart.

He plants his feet on the glossy wooden steps. His pace to approach a cowering me is steady. My shame is visible to everyone in this glorious throne room. It makes my skin itch the way I cry in front of these strong-minded people. Silent tears still travel down my face.

"You have broken the very honor code you sought after. You kept a secret that came close to killing your fellow knights. Why should I give you mercy?" His voice is unnaturally calm. There's a hint of pain lingering in his words as well.

This is my last chance to prove myself to King Kasper and all of Thrallen. I'm not going to waste it. Not after meeting my younger brother.

I'm lucky the massive ceilings carry my womanly tone out to the knights and townsfolk.

"The written laws of Thrallen have nothing against women going after knighthood. Only acceptable if those women are of noble birth." I turn around to face the people. Some don't meet my eyes. I'm going to make them listen either way.

"I am from a village where no noblemen live. Yes, I lied about my birth. But if I had been noble, you all would have laughed in my face. My idea of being a knight would be silly to you. What else was I to do?" I make sure to catch wandering gazes. I'm speaking my truth.

"So, I decided to dress myself like a man. I only wanted to become a knight. It was all I've wanted my whole life. I was going to be denied it either way. I didn't care what I would have to do to get it. Me sacrificing myself to keep the king safe must be enough. I earned my knighthood." Slowly, I twist back to meet Kasper's gaze.

I swallow deeply before continuing. "I proved myself repeatedly. I risked my life to save you. I would do it all again. This is who I am. I deserve to be a knight. Don't take away my dream when I only just grasped onto it."

My words seem to touch everyone's heart. Sniffs and whispers fill the hall quickly. I never lied to take advantage of the kingdom. Only to earn my destiny.

King Kasper glances at his people of different colors and backgrounds. Not one person is the same. And yet they come together in times of need. I can only hope he understands everything I said.

But then he speaks.

"Anna Scarrow is the child thought to be murdered by my

father." He announces loudly to his people. Shock rolls across the hall.

That does not stop his voice. "Her mother was Queen Pearlina. Anna's father was my own. She is my sister. I cannot cast her out after just finding her. It would not be very kingly of me."

Then he decides to turn my world upside down. "She will remain a Knight of Thrallen forevermore. Due to her heroic actions, I hear by request my sister to become the crowned princess of Thrallen. And that is that."

A gasp of relief spills from my lips. I drop to my knees in fits of sobs. The warlock is at my side in an instant. Crowlen helps me back to my feet to face the king again. I welcome Crowlen's tight and possessive hands that find their place on my sides.

Kasper rips me from Crowlen and takes me into his arms. I'm still in shock that we share the same blood. I have to be at least a year or two older than him. There is no sure way of knowing. It doesn't matter.

"I failed the knights and you. How must I fix this?" My words are muffled into his chest. Kasper brings up a hand to smooth out my hair. His slight chuckle causes my eardrums to shake.

It has to be strange for him to have family of his once again in these halls. Maybe my presence will further brighten this world around him.

"You are my sister. We glorious Madlock royals always find a way to make things right. Have faith in yourself, sister." King Kasper beams.

Me and my brother, the king, walk up the steps.

The knights instantly stand straight in their formation at

the front of the hall. "Long live the Madlock tree." They all chant three times.

As if claiming an oath to me and Kasper. I feel powerful in their loyalty. Kasper and I take it all in, absorbing it through our fingers and ears. Facing down the people as they dance around in glory. Music now fills the room with heavy notes that soothe my worries.

The owners of the Yellow Piggle tell their story of how they housed the lost princess to those who requested it.

Crowlen who shares my soul watches me like a hawk. Making sure I'm not planning to vanish. Well, he doesn't have to worry about that.

I knew I always belonged somewhere special. I've found my forever home. It's the kingdom of Thrallen.

I am a Knight of Thrallen like I was always meant to be. It's safe to say that my father would be proud of me. Let's hope I can continue pushing forward.

Bonus Chapter

Dreams are always meant to be lodged deep into a person's mind. Locked away until someone eventually forgets about them. Taken by the Seekers themselves to the blazing pits of the underplace.

And yet I defied every odd the Seekers threw at me and became a knight by pure determination.

I might have once dreamed of such things. Looking up at the brown broken ceiling in my father's little cabin as I grew older. Thinking of how nice it would be to become a Knight of Thrallen.

Now it has really happened. A reality that I can now sulk in whenever I wish.

My dream came true. I did everything in my power to make it so. Even killing myself in the process. Well, that was an accident. Though I did get rid of an evil queen despite sharing blood with that woman.

Which I will still need time to get over. It's not every day that I find out I'm related to a real witch.

So why do my fellow knights continue to belittle my journey to this point in my life? They make fun of the way my wrists jolt to the side during rank training sessions. Even gripe about how my height makes me a child compared to them all.

I won't ever understand how such terrible men can simply poke at me silly. Isn't it in the knight's code to love all and forever protect the royal family? Yes, and somehow that doesn't seem to count when it comes to me.

I didn't think anyone was supposed to get special attention. Least of all me.

It takes great internal strength not to lash out when they sometimes walk behind me and snicker. Their words are so obvious. They're able to carry on the winds that continue to drift through the creeping fall. Turns out that it was Pearlina who made the weather go cold in Thrallen only. A war tactic that hasn't been used since the Battle of Doom. Eventually, summer came around, and now softer winds have rolled in.

I hear them talk of my strange hair. The way my battered sword awkwardly glints in the sunlight. A scouting party that had been sent to uncover lost armor had found it hidden behind a boulder. I claimed it in the Lost and Found hut at the front gates.

None of it seems original. Their conversations are always about the same fucking things. It's getting tiring just hearing about it over and over again.

It's been almost four months since King Kasper declared me as his bastard sister. Telling everyone that I will eventually be crowned princess of Thrallen.

Why must they mess around with me still? Sometimes I wonder if they were bored before the battle against Pearlina. Maybe I offer them new entertainment.

I can't believe that they even dare to say one word about me. They show me no true ounce of respect. None of these brute men can offer me a polite smile whenever we cross paths. It's like they purposely go out of their way to ruin my day.

I hear the little whispers that fly throughout the castle when my back is turned. Kitchen staff saying how I forced my village to fund my rough travels. The messengers in training even say that I tricked Artis into lodging.

I'm sure it was the knights who fed into these rumors. There is no other explanation.

Well, if I know one thing for sure it's that I won't let them win this battle.

That's why I wield my mighty sword on the training grounds before the misty dawn. I don't rack my bow and quiver of arrows until an hour after sunset. Making sure I outlast every other man who dares to train beside me.

Meaning I will forever train with this old knight's instructor. Sir Charlie isn't very into training these days though. It's a wonder how he can still stand. Even if that suggests to others that I'm a little unhinged.

~ ~ ~

I draw back my hand and let the cool steel of the small dagger bite into my shaking flesh. I inhale sharply as the afternoon sun shines down into my irritated eyes.

Sweat drips between my eyes from off my wet brows. I swear harshly under my breath. The dagger continues slipping as I fight hard to keep my jittery position.

I've been losing sleep these past few nights. Thoughts of the not-so-distant past force me awake. Flashes of the recent murder I committed haunt me like a fresh ghost.

Sometimes I cry out as I thrust my hands forward. Releasing

my fingers to allow the slightly curved silver blade to jolt through the slightly chilled air.

The dagger, however, strikes true. Right in the middle of the mead barrel lid that has been painted to look like another target. It hits right in the middle with a gut-twisting thud. My throw is so hard that the lid cracks all down the middle, threatening to break in half.

My constant training has drained me of all glee. I can't even sport a smile. There is no time for getting excited. So, I move to the nearest bench and pick up another dagger with a leather hilt. I'm fully prepared to throw it as well.

But my entire body gets ridged when I hear someone's boots crunch on the dead grass behind me. I clench my jaw tightly. My lungs squeeze inward.

I jerk around. Fully expected to find an empty field. All the other knights cleared out. None dare to join me. No one ever bothers to invite me to a sparring match.

There's someone slowly approaching me. Holding his large hands up high. Letting me know he isn't here to harm me.

I squint my eyes suspiciously. Not fully trusting whoever this is. I cross my aching arms. Breathing slowly to calm my racing heart.

"Do you ever give yourself a break?" The newcomer asks. A knight a little older than me.

He has cropped brown hair. Not very shiny looking. But the very tips curled just a tad. His eyes are the color of honey. An innocent shade that I try my best to welcome.

My gaze drops a little. I step back a few feet. Not totally sure what this knight expects of me.

"I realize some of us knights aren't very subtle when it comes to gossip. Is there anything I can do to help make it stop?" The man who wears the same armor as me has guilt shimmering across his eyes.

I don't want his pity. I'd rather die back in that battle against Pearlina than have people think me useless.

I lift my gaze, making our eyes lock. I want to make sure he can see the fire that burns within my soul that isn't fully mine anymore. Plus, this red eye of mine tends to glow at every turn as my anger spikes. I got that from Crowlen. Duh.

"You all may not like how I went about my knighthood, but I have it. I fought for it with all my might. If you have a problem, then I suggest you take it up with me personally. You can tell your men that if you'd wish." I hiss through gritted teeth.

The man who stands in front of me actually smiles in response. His face lights up brightly. The setting sun makes his tan skin shine.

"I was also a competitor in the Knight Trials. I am the fourth-born son of House Maxter. Not even my own mother and father and three older brothers thought I could win my place within the Thrallen ranks. You are not alone in the boat of feeling unworthy of the title." His words hurt me almost.

That's when I realize I'm not the only one who risked everything to become a knight. I often struggle with seeing the outside picture. Perhaps it's a good idea to expand my mind to those around me.

I nod for him to continue, letting loose hair fly across my forehead.

"My noble family has the royal right to be knights without having to work for it. But I always knew I wanted to earn my knighthood. I understand what you fought for, Anna Scarrow." He shrugs his shoulders like it's nothing.

It's the first time I ever felt helpless. At least in the sense of

239

emotion.

I offer him a trembling hand. "I'm Anna Scarrow, She Knight of Thrallen. Hopefully, the first of many more to come." My next step in the future is encouraging more women to join the ranks.

The other knight grips my arm, pulling me a little tighter. A massive grin is on his perfect rosy lips.

"Sir Borren, a pleasure to meet you, She Knight." His fingers dig into my hands, but I don't care. I just found a friend in this new messy world.

We drift apart. Sir Borren suggests a quick sparring match with wooden swords. I can't find it in my heart to say no.

I never knew how much I needed a friend until now.

Maybe it's the Seeker's way of letting me know that I'm not the only one who was dealt with really complicated cards.

It's somewhat hard having my father around. Not being able to tell him of my plans for the future is rather sad. I can't even show him the few aspen trees that are scattered about in the woods.

But what am I to do now? What would Ceden Scarrow tell me that I should be doing after all this?

Probably along the lines of, *"The present journey might be over. However, there is always more to follow behind."*

He was a man of many wise words. I still sneak around with various weapons inside my boots and underneath my clothing. One can never be too prepared.

As I grin brightly and clash the wooden sword against Sir Borren's. I imagine my father is there standing off to the side. Cheering me on as I playfully jab my newest friend in the side.

"You sure know your way around the sword!" Sir Borren yelps while trying his best to get out of the way.

I twist around to make sure he fails to slice my armor-clad shoulder.

"I've been working my ass off," I exclaim rather fondly. I lift my sore arms high in the air in triumph. Clearly, I have already beaten Sir Borren in this match.

A throaty laugh escapes him. "I think we shall be great friends, She Knight."

I release a deep breath as I plop my sword onto the ground. "We shall see what tomorrow brings us."

My hands ache from gripping the wooden hilt so damn tight. My heart is speeding greatly. And yet I'm no longer feeling sorry for myself. No sadness coats my spirit either.

I shall from now on convince myself to be grateful for everything that has come my way.

I'm going to learn to live my life here in Thrallen with half of my soul being shared with the warlock. I will give this knighthood all that I have in me.

Another Bonus Chapter

"Are you sure you can't feel him anymore?" Aunty Kurty wipes down a few tables while I continue to sulk. I note how dirty the surfaces are after a hunting party fled the tavern to beat the upcoming storm.

They left soiled cloths and smudged mugs halfway empty of ale. Some never returned their basket of peanuts either. Sometimes I wish Kurty was firmer with them about at least trying to clean after themselves.

I scoff as a rumble of thunder sounds off deep in the distance. Letting the noise rattle my insides like an old bell.

"It's like one side of my being is numb constantly. I'm sure he's done something to keep me from feeling his power. But why?" I rub my face vigorously. My tired eyes struggle to keep me awake. If I close them for a single second too long, then I'll be snoozing.

I stayed out later on the training grounds than I wanted to. I of course outlasted Sir Borren. He usually stays by my side the best he can. Not even he could keep up with me on this night.

Kurty sighs heavily and tosses down the damp washing cloth.

I tend to find humor in the way she puffs her large chest when she readies to give me a stern talking-to.

"Perhaps he doesn't want you to experience his feelings for you?" Her suggestion paired with her wiggling brows throws me into a chuckling whirl.

Unwillingly, I gasp in fright as a big flash of blue lightning crosses the dark sky. The bright light is a unique flame shining through the gloomy windows at the front of the tavern. It's a shock to me. I didn't expect to be grazed with a bolt of lightning the size of that one.

It shines through the open window and illuminates all the walls of the Yellow Piggle. Almost setting the entire place ablaze. Somehow, I find it soothing.

"Oh, I'm sure Thrallen's warlock doesn't feel anything for me other than hate, disgust, and anger. He probably has so much of it that he shields it away, so it won't kill me in an instant. There can't be no other explanation." I stifle a laugh under a groan.

I'm very aware that Kurty looks upon me with grand uncertainty. Like she's debating whether to hag me or wring my neck into a tight twist. Neither option is appealing.

The much older woman takes a seat at the table she had just cleaned. Gazing upon me from where I sit at the bar with my small hands clutching a now warm glass of ale. I fail to keep my head held high.

"Anna, you think so little of yourself." The woman says. Pity coats her words. A knowing glint in her eyes.

A groan flees my lips as I square my shoulders. The thick knitted sweater I'm wearing keeps the warmth wrapped around my body perfectly. And yet I still can't stop my spine from shivering.

I take a large gulp of my drink. "I have no idea what you're talking about."

I refuse to believe in myself in such ways. I'm not like that. Am I? Seekers, no!

Kurty shakes her head. She clearly doesn't like my answer.

"That crease in your forehead hasn't eased since you went through the first Knight Trial." I had no idea Kurty pays that much attention to me.

This discovery causes me to shift uncomfortably on the barstool. I tuck my bruised hands into the pockets of my sweater. Grasping onto an invisible strand of longing.

"I'm fine," I speak softly. Afraid that if my voice is any higher then I might potentially lash out.

But I know that it's a lie. I was never a person to keep things to myself. Though this isn't something I'm ready to talk about. Especially not with Aunty Kurty or Artis. Perhaps not ever.

Kurty nods her head slowly. Then chooses her next words carefully. "I may not remember how a young woman's mind works, but I do know that love is a complicated thing. I'd be careful."

I seize quickly. A bright flush spreads to my neck and face. My words stumble out of my mouth in a troublesome rush.

"You are insane, Kurty." I don't believe what this woman says. Of course, I'm not in love with Crowlen. That is the most ridiculous thing I've ever heard. I laugh to myself the whole way back to the castle after Kurty shooed me out of the Yellow Piggle.

I'm glad the chilling rain quickly gets rid of the unwanted heat in my bones before I make it to the castle doors.

Book Two

THE THRALLEN SAGA

PROTECT OUR KNIGHT

HARLIE HARGRAVES

Prologue of Protect Our Knight

Finely done portraits hang along the lengthy dark wooden wall. Dim colors of gray and orange and yellow carefully had once been painted across thin canvases.

The perfectly drawn-out pictures were placed in golden frames lined with ivory pearls. Dust collects right on the tops of their frames, creating a fluffy stripe. Each work is precisely aligned with one another. Someone must have really wanted these pictures to be the center of everyone's attention.

Nothing is out of place.

I have walked past these pictures every day since my brother, the king, claimed me as the princess. And yet I never had the desire to gaze upon them. They honestly mean nothing to me.

None of the people in these photos are my family.

They are just some dreadful art hanging around a wide hall.

But today's walk feels different for once.

I was compelled to stop and grace my eyes over every single one. Their faces are pale and lifeless. I have a sudden desire to understand why royal families insisted on capturing their horrid expressions in such a way.

As if they possessed no soul.

How awful that is.

They're all the same in many ways. Each painted king wore royal brown and yellow robes. That beautiful crown sitting atop their heads. The shining green jewel blasted through the darkness that is the Madlock family. Even their eyes happened to be the same color. Ocean blue just like Kasper's.

Unforgettable.

Magical.

Dangerous.

I don't seem to get how that's possible. The same shade. The same narrowness. Of course, their lashes were thick and long and blonde. Those noses were small and pointed.

Like they're copies of each other. Total replicas of themselves that couldn't have been a coincidence. It's eerie.

I can't find anything I have in common with any of them.

Maybe I don't want to pick out similar features. I never knew these kings. Certainly not the late Dragoona Madlock. His portrait is the farthest one on the right. Its paint is still exposed to dry. The smell of these thick oil colors drifts in the air.

The urge to drag my fingertips across the canvas chews at the back of my mind. I force myself to keep my hands behind my chocolate brown cape.

I walk down the hall slowly to face the picture. A slight tremor enters my chest.

Dragoona really did look like his son. Though Kasper is definitely more friendly, certainly more handsome. This makes me squirm in my knight armor. It's hard to imagine that I too am the late king's sire.

No one sane can guess that. We have nothing in common.

I try to picture us all together in the great hall. Laughing with joy. As a true family. But it ends in terror, covered in tragic power. Like it was never meant to be. The worst part of this silly fantasy is that I can't imagine a mother by our side.

Dragoona passed of old age. Kasper's mother died while giving birth to him a year after Queen Pearlina seduced the king. It's all a mess that I just want to put behind me.

Something that me and Kasper have in common at least.

Mother figures aren't supposed to be in our lives. The damn Seekers made sure of it.

I'm still a little shaken up about knowing I am actually related to an evil witch.

To me, there is no resemblance. I take after my mother. Well, my real mother. The one who had been married to my late father and died before I could even remember her. I have my mother's hazel eyes. Or at least I used to.

Strange to consider that my father lied about my true origins. Ceden Scarrow was the greatest man I have ever known. Nothing is going to change that.

~ ~ ~

Warm air floats down the corridor. It disturbs my long white hair to expose the points of my ears. Letting the empty world know of my magical features.

The desire to linger around this hall fades away like an old memory.

I need to step away before my mind becomes overwhelmed with distant possibilities. After all, I have much more important things to do other than stare at old men for the rest of the day.

There is always something to do within this wonderful city.

Such as aiding my fellow knights in keeping the Kingdom of Thrallen safe and sound.

About the Author

Harlie Hargraves lives in Texas with her family and many pets. She has an associate's degree in General Academics (liberal arts pathway). Her favorite genre of books is horror and fantasy. Though she is very much into monster romance. She particularly likes the Indiana Jones movies and favors The Hobbit.